Estrella's Quinceañera

Estrella's Quinceañera

Malín Alegría

SIMON & SCHUSTER BOOKS FOR YOUNG READERS
New York   London   Toronto   Sydney

"Spanglish 101," a glossary, begins on page 255.

SIMON & SCHUSTER BOOKS FOR YOUNG READERS

An imprint of Simon & Schuster Children's Publishing Division
1230 Avenue of the Americas, New York, New York 10020

SIMON & SCHUSTER BOOKS FOR YOUNG READERS is a trademark
of Simon & Schuster, Inc.

Produced by Alloy Entertainment
151 West 26th Street, New York, NY 10001

Book design by Amy Trombat
The text for this book is set in Scala.
Manufactured in the United States of America
4 6 8 10 9 7 5 3
Library of Congress Cataloging-in-Publication Data
Alegría, Malín.
Estrella's quinceañera / Malín Alegría.— 1st ed.
p. cm.
Summary: Estrella's mother and aunt are planning a gaudy, traditional quinceañera for
her, even though it is the last thing she wants.
ISBN-13: 978-0-689-87809-1 (isbn 13)
ISBN-10: 0-689-87809-5 (isbn 10)
1. Mexican Americans—Juvenile fiction. [1. Mexican Americans—Fiction.
2. Quinceañera (Social custom)—Fiction. 3. Mothers and daughters—Fiction.
4. Friendship—Fiction.] I. Title.
PZ7.A37338Est 2006
[Fic]—dc22
2005014540

*To all the girls who are trying to find their own path.
May your journey be lit with bellyaching laughs, crazy
adventures, and a fierce commitment to your dreams.*

Estrella's Quinceañera

quinceañera (keen-see-ah-'nyair-ah) n., Spanish, formal (quince ['keen-say] for short): 1. traditional party (one that I refuse to have). According to my mom, a girl's fifteenth birthday is supposed to be the biggest day in her life. The quinceañera is like a huge flashing neon sign for womanhood. Back in olden times, it meant that a woman was ready to get married and have babies. 2. The way I see it, it's just a lame party with cheesy music and puffy princess dresses.

C'MON, SHORTY," BOBBY SAID, while pulling me into the conga line.

"This is ridiculous!" I yelled over the deafening music. I gripped my brother's shirt tightly.

"Don't be such a nerd, Estrella," he joked with a cheesy grin. "This is a fiesta."

But it wasn't just any party. This was Teresa Sandoval's *quinceañera*, the biggest day of her life—or at least that's what our mothers told us. Tere had gone all out, cha-cha style. She was dancing at the front of the conga line in a white, layered dress with puffy sleeves. A rhinestone-studded tiara was balanced on top of her head. Tere looked like she was getting married, but there was no groom, just a bunch of pimply-faced cousins dressed in extra-large black suits.

"Don't be jealous," said Rey, my other brother. He and Bobby were both seventeen, fraternal twins but identically annoying. He cut in behind me and held my waist as the line wove around an oval table.

"I'm not jealous!"

Rey snickered behind me. Okay, so the Hyatt was kind of cool, and Tere did get to ride around in a white limo all day. But whatever—the reception was totally tacky. The decorations looked like rejects from the flea market, lace and frills everywhere. And what was up with the pathetic lime-green balloons rolling all over the floor? Couldn't anyone get it together to find a helium tank?

But from the looks of all the happy people conga-ing with me, I seemed to be the only one who had noticed.

"So when did Tere become so hot?" Rey asked.

I turned around and looked at Tere. Her hair had been twirled into ringlets that were pinned on top of her head. A few tendrils hung down and framed her face. Her skin was clear and smooth. She had recently grown boobs—big ones. She looked nothing like the chubby kid who used to come over to my house and play Connect Four. We'd been so close then; she'd come over practically every day after school. But we weren't friends anymore. Technically, I hadn't even been invited to this party.

When Tere's invitation had come in the mail, everyone in my family had been listed but me. My mom said it was probably just a mistake and insisted I come anyway. I, of course, knew that it was one hundred percent intentional, but I didn't have the heart to explain that to my mother. So I came. And now here I was, feeling anxious, hoping that maybe, just maybe, Tere wouldn't notice me.

The mariachi music picked up and people started running to catch up with the group. But it was too fast for my eighty-year-old nana. She slipped and fell, letting out a whooping laugh as she landed on the ground.

I felt instantly embarrassed. Not for my nana—she seemed to be having a grand old time right where she was—but for myself. I tried to imagine how this would look to Sheila and Christie—the overly frilly decorations, the sad balloons, and in the middle of it all, a tiny, wrinkly little old lady cackling on the floor. I felt my face grow hot. The music ended and everyone broke out in cheers for the *quinceañera*.

Bobby ran over to Nana, who was still clapping and laughing on the floor. She was having a merry time. *Oh my God!* I thought as Bobby reached out for her. Bobby was a pretty big guy and I was afraid he might dislocate her arm if he pulled her up too quickly. But he also had a soft streak that always surprised me whenever it appeared. He gently helped Nana to her feet and led her to a chair.

Nana shook her head. She didn't want to sit. I'd caught her sipping champagne earlier at our table, and I knew she would not go quietly. She grabbed Bobby by the hips and started shimmying her shoulders. Rey started to cheer from the sidelines.

"Go Bobby! Go Nana!"

I couldn't help but smile while I watched Bobby's face turn bright red. One thing about Mexican parties: they're always a lot of fun. If only I could have gotten into the spirit of things. I turned around and saw my mom sitting with my dad at our table. She was waving frantically at me.

"Be right back," I called out to Rey as I made my way through screaming kids and dancing couples.

My mother smiled as I approached. People said we looked alike, but I didn't see the resemblance. Okay, so I had her petite frame, kinky black hair, and pretty lips, but that's where it ended. We were totally different about things like fashion, makeup, and hairstyles. I cared about them (a lot) and my mother didn't (at all). In her fuchsia dress (two sizes two big, complete with giant shoulder pads), my mom was a serious candidate for one of those TV fashion emergency shows. But I had to admit, I loved seeing her face light up and her dark eyes twinkle. Ever since we'd arrived she'd been ooohing and aahing over everything: the ruffles, the cake, Tere's dress, those sad balloons. Just another example of how different we really were.

My dad, Manuel, who everyone called Manny for short, kept looking at his watch. He was missing the San Francisco Giants game and wasn't happy about it. He reached out for the half-full bottle of Bacardi that sat in the middle of the table as if it were a centerpiece. He took a few long gulps. Like me, he was just there to please my mother. He looked up and gave me a wink. We were in this together.

"*Mija*," my mom said as I sat down next to her. She handed

me a paper napkin containing Nana's coffee-stained dentures.

"Gross!" I tossed them onto the table.

"I told Nana that she couldn't eat the cake until it was served, and then," she sighed, throwing a napkin over the teeth, "I found these by the cake."

The image of Nana sneaking some cake like a naughty little kid was so funny that my dad and I burst out laughing.

"This is not a joke." My mother tried to hold back a smile. "If anyone saw those teeth, I don't know what I'd do."

"Don't worry, Mom." I took the napkin-wrapped dentures in my hand. "I'll make sure these go back in her mouth and that she stays far away from the dessert."

My mom gave me a kiss on the cheek before I wound my way back into the mob of bobbing heads and swinging hips on the dance floor. Nana and Bobby had disappeared from the spot where I'd left them, so I began to weave through tables and head toward the cake—just in case Nana wanted to go for seconds.

"Hey, Estrella."

I turned and smiled into the cheerful face of my cousin Marta, who was sitting with her two babies, Temo and Maya. Maya had fallen fast asleep, despite the loud music. She looked so cute in her frilly baby-blue dress. Four-year-old Temo was in this tiny little baby-size brown tux, eating a piece of cake. I ran over and covered him with kisses. It felt like years since I'd seen him.

"Oh my God! I can't believe you're here," I said, giving Marta a big hug. She looked very mom-ish in her cream floral dress, with heavy bags under her eyes. Marta was always my favorite cousin. She was like the older sister I never had, but I hadn't seen her in a while. Four years ago, Marta had "tarnished" (according to her mother) the entire family's reputation when she'd gotten pregnant, dropped out of school, and shacked up with Suave, who my mother always used to call "that *Vago* with the black Camaro." A few months ago, Marta and Suave had finally gotten married at city hall, and now they lived in a tiny apartment in Cupertino with their two kids. Marta's relationship with her mother, my *tía* Lucky, was awful at best, and Marta wasn't invited to family functions anymore.

"Well, I think the whole city was invited," Marta joked as she looked around the packed room. The Gonzalezes were dancing with the Veras. *Señora* Vera had been a well-known dancer back in Mexico City. Even though she was almost as old as my nana, she was still the best dancer at the party. The Ortizes, the Talamateses, and the Montoyas were sitting at a table eating cake. The Ruizes were laughing hysterically at the Hugo and Margarita Martinez table, probably over one of Hugo's famous impersonations. He was one of my father's best friends and could make his voice sound like anyone's—even mine. Pedro Dominguez and Ernesto Lopez were toasting Tere with bottles of Corona. The list went on. These were the people I'd known all my life, and being with everyone together like this made me feel safe and suffocated at the same time.

"Did you say hi to my mom? She's right over there." I pointed toward the exit. "*Tía* Lucky should be over there, too."

Marta shrugged and fiddled with the napkin on her lap.

"Oh, come on, Marta," I said, tugging on her arm. "Why don't you just go over and say hi?"

Marta shook her head. "Maybe next time. I should be going. It's getting late."

"Oh, don't be like that." When we were in public, *Tía* Lucky and Marta just ignored each other. But behind closed doors my *tía* ranted about what an ungrateful, good-for-nothing daughter she was. Marta wasn't helping anything by staying away.

Marta got up and started getting Temo ready to go. He was still eating his cake and began to cry, waving his arms and legs. He kicked over a vase of red and yellow flowers with his tiny little dress shoe. Water spread out all over the white lace tablecloth.

"Why don't you just wait until he's finished? What's the hurry?"

Marta gave me a cold look that told me to butt out. She mopped up the water with a blue napkin.

"Well," I said, turning away slowly, "nice seeing you."

I wished Marta and her mother would make peace. Their fighting meant I hardly ever got to see Marta, and I really missed her. Even so, I understood Marta's desire to keep her distance. After all, I had spent the entire party trying to avoid Tere and Izzy.

Unfortunately, I was on a mission to find Nana, and it didn't look like I could avoid Tere anymore. There she was, standing in front of the three-tiered white cake, passing out extra-thin slices to everyone. She had some frosting in her ringlets and on her cheek. Someone had shoved cake in her face, which was a family tradition. I was sorry I'd missed that. It was always my favorite part of a party. There was a group of girls in matching dresses standing with Tere, giggling and whispering to her.

Obviously these were Tere's *damas*, her female escorts. *Girls always choose their best friends as* damas *in order to celebrate this special occasion together*, I thought with a pang of regret. Once I was sure Nana wasn't around, I decided to head back to my family's table.

"Watch it!" a girl hissed as she bumped into my shoulder.

"Sorry," I said. Then I looked up into the dark, fiery eyes of Isabel Flores. Izzy hated her name and refused to answer to Isabel. She was tough, the kind of girl who wasn't scared of anything. She never worried about getting hassled by thugs in our neighborhood. They made my walk home miserable with incessant catcalls, but they didn't mess with Izzy. They were probably worried about getting hassled by *her*! She wore scuffed army boots, a long trench coat, and a sparkly black flower pinned into her hair (which was probably her attempt at dressing up).

Izzy gave me a nasty smirk. "Well, you have nerve, showing up here." She and I were also super-close childhood friends. Or rather, had been. "Can't return a phone call for eight months, but you're quick to show up at a party. I see how it is."

"Whatever," I mumbled and shoved my way past her toward my family's table.

"Why don't you go hang out with your rich bitch private school friends?" she called out behind me. I felt my stomach tighten. It wasn't as if I didn't feel bad for what had happened between us, but some of it hadn't been my fault.

Last year, I'd been lucky enough to win an academic scholarship to Sacred Heart, this upscale high school in the wealthiest part of San Jose. I'd been busting my butt there, trying to keep my grades up. . . . So yeah, I guess you could say I'd been blowing Tere and Izzy off. And if I was being honest about it, there was another reason, too—I'd also been hanging out with a couple of Sacred Heart girls, Christie and Sheila, who just *happened* to be white and just *happened* to have a lot of money. Being around them made me feel alive and free to do whatever and be whomever I wanted. I guess, as lame as it might sound, sometimes what I wanted was to be just like them.

Izzy joined Tere's group of girls and I walked back to the table. Nana was sitting between Bobby and Rey, eating cake alarmingly fast for someone without teeth. My mom's baby sister, *Tía* Lucky, had joined us and was checking out all the eligible men over forty.

I plopped into my seat.

"Tere hooked us up with extra cake," Bobby said, grinning. "I think she likes me."

"Whatever," Rey cut in. "She just gave you the parts Nana stuck her finger in."

"Gross," I said.

My mother covered my hand with hers. "Isn't this beautiful, Estrella?" She was watching the DJ's light show on the dance floor.

I glanced at my watch. "I guess." *If you like tacky stuff,* I thought, sighing at the sight of my *tía's* neon-green spandex dress and bright purple eye shadow.

"*Mija,*" my mother said, "this is a *quinceañera*. They're supposed to be big. That's part of the fun! Now, when you have yours . . ."

No, I thought as my heartbeat began to race.

She and I had already had this discussion a month ago. I'd told her that I didn't want one. In truth, just thinking about it made my face feel hot. Nobody at my school had a *quinceañera*. I'd be surprised if any of them knew what one was.

"Mom, but you said . . . ," I began. She'd promised me that I didn't have to have a *quince* if I really didn't want to. She couldn't flip the script on me now. But she looked so hopeful, and she was practically vibrating with excitement, so I swallowed my words. It was the same look she got when she saw a bargain at a garage sale. I decided to try a different tack.

"You know, having a *quinceañera* is really expensive and kind of a waste of money, don't you think? Maybe it would be better if—"

But she didn't even let me finish. "*Mija*," my mother protested lovingly, "do not worry about the money. Even if we *were* worried about the money, we could always get *padrinos* to help us pay. This is tradition. Our tradition is what keeps us grounded. It reminds us of who we are. Just because we don't live in Mexico doesn't mean we're not Mexican. You can call yourself anything you want—Chicano, Latino, whatever—but your roots never change. It's our blood. This is more important than the money. What better thing is there to spend money on?"

I tried to keep myself from rolling my eyes. I'd heard this speech at least a million times before.

"Can't we compromise?" I asked hopefully. "Let's rent a club downtown. We can have mariachis!"

My mother gave me a funny look, like she had just been insulted. "This is not about mariachis."

"No, it's definitely not," *Tía* Lucky added.

I wished *Tía* would just mind her own business. Of course, that would never happen in my lifetime. My dad and brothers were unusually quiet. I turned to them in a plea for help, but they looked away. I was on my own.

"This is about tradition," my mother continued.

"And the church," Lucky chimed in.

"Family."

"Heritage."

"Culture."

"Obligation!" Nana added, raising one cake-covered finger in the air.

My mother reached out and grabbed my hand. "When I was your age, only the rich girls had *quinceañeras*. I've dreamed of this day since the doctor told me you would be a girl." She pinched my cheek. "Everything will be fine. You'll see." She looked back at the dance floor. The lights had dimmed and couples were slow-dancing to a *bolero*. "You're going to love it."

I felt something tighten in my chest when I saw the way she was gazing out at the party. How could I say no? "Okay, Mom." I knew I was going to regret this. "Just promise me that it'll be a small one."

"I promise," she said. Then she pulled me into a tight hug. There was something almost desperate about it, as if she was afraid that at any second, I'd just disappear.

> **estrella** (es-'tray-ah) n., Spanish, formal: 1. English translation: star 2. My parents named me Estrella because I was born on a starry night. They also say that I am the star of their lives. 3. Everyone at school calls me Star because I hate the way the nuns say "Iz-tree-lah," like my name is a tongue twister or something.

ON THAT WARM APRIL EVENING, my mom drove our Dodge minivan slowly up the street toward Sheila's Mediterranean-style home in Willow Glen. The car was a huge eyesore, with duct tape covering the broken taillight and key scratches along the left side. I was glad it was dark and no one could see it.

Thanks to my mom, I was already an hour late. After Tere's party my mother had insisted on dropping off my dad and brothers at the house, making sure Nana took her medication, brainstorming with *Tía* Lucky about *quince* preparations, and getting gas for the car. In the Alvarez family, my needs always came last. There was always an emergency—someone needed a ride, had good gossip to share, or was complaining that something had broken down. But it was worth the wait. Now I could hang with Christie and Sheila. When I was with them, I felt far away from *quinceañeras* and frilliness and missing dentures. When the three of us were together, I felt like I could be someone else.

"*Mija*," my mother said as she pulled up to Sheila's wrought-iron gate, "do you want me to walk in with you?" She was craning her neck, trying to get a better view of the two-story house that was hidden behind a cluster of willow trees and beautifully landscaped bushes.

I quickly gave her a peck on the cheek and jumped out of the car. "I'll be okay."

"I just think it's funny that I've never met your friends."

"Next time, I promise. Right now, I'm so late," I said, slamming the car door closed.

"Call me when you want me to pick you up, okay? In the morning, I'm going to Margarita's," she said. Margarita was one of her oldest friends and the owner of Taquería 2000, a local Mexican restaurant. "But after that I will come home and wait for you to call."

"Don't worry about it. I'll take the bus tomorrow," I said and waved as she drove away.

We went through the same thing every time she dropped me off. Part of me felt like of course my mother should get to meet my friends. Before I'd started going to Sacred Heart, she'd known every kid in my class by first and last name. But an even bigger part of me cringed with embarrassment at the mere idea of bringing my mother into Sheila's nice house.

The truth was, my mother always embarrassed me. The first week at Sacred Heart, she'd shown up in her house clothes. I'd forgotten my homework on the table. When she left, I heard a couple of girls snicker and make comments about the maid's daughter—which I knew were directed at me. I'd never felt so humiliated before in my life. Things had never been like that when I went to public school, because everyone's mother dressed like that. I opened the gate and ran up the lit cobblestone pathway to Sheila's house.

"Star!" Sheila yelled from the doorway. I felt better already. Seeing Tere and Izzy again had brought back all these unresolved feelings of guilt about the way I'd dissed them. But one look at Sheila standing there—her hands on her tiny hips, trying to look mad while sucking on a Blow Pop—made me burst into giggles. "And where have you been, young lady?" Sheila took the blue Blow Pop out of her mouth and shook it at me in mock disapproval.

"Ugh. I cannot even *begin* to tell you. My parents made me go to this totally lame party. I couldn't get out of it."

We hugged.

"Sorry," I said over her shoulder.

"Excuses, excuses." She leaned back from the hug and wrinkled her small straight nose. "Well, I don't know what sort of crazy parties your family likes to go to, honey, but you smell like a roasted pig."

I suddenly felt embarrassed, remembering how Bobby and Rey had thought it was so hilarious to toss little pieces of *carnitas* at my head at the *quince*. The scent must have stuck to me.

"Oh, yeah. Ha," I forced myself to laugh, but it came out sounding like a cough.

"Where's Christie?" I asked, taking off my coat in the foyer. Sheila lived in my dream house. Her mother was an art dealer and had the hottest collection of paintings, Indian pottery, and crafts I'd ever seen. Sheila's mom was a cool Indiana Jones type who scavenged the earth for rare antique pieces. She was always traveling to foreign places and bringing Sheila back the most amazing gifts. Their house was like a museum, and usually I was scared that I was going to break something.

"Where else?" Sheila replied, crossing her arms. "She's on the phone with Mark."

I rolled my eyes.

"Has she no shame?" I asked as we climbed the stairs to Sheila's room on the second floor. The house was way too big for two people, but it was beautifully decorated in a rustic Southwest and Asian Zen–style decor. Sheila had the entire second floor basically to herself. It was ridiculous, but I loved it.

"She's been on her cell all night. I don't even know why she bothered to come." Sheila said harshly. I liked Sheila's straight-up, no-nonsense attitude. The fact that we were both new to Sacred Heart made our bond tighter.

Sheila had transferred in midyear from a boarding school in Mendocino. Apparently, this was her third transfer since beginning high school. She complained that the kids out there were a bunch of Birkenstock brats who got high all the time. They couldn't appreciate her humor. Her mom moved her to Sacred Heart after she ran away for the umpteenth time. "All I wanted was a decent burger," she'd explain.

"The last thing I heard Christie say was, 'Tell me how much you love me, Mookie-Pants.'"

"Oh my goodness." I made a gagging noise.

Sheila grabbed my hand. "Promise me, Star, that when you get a boyfriend, you won't forget the little people who made you who you are."

I laughed and then frowned. That kind of talk just reminded me of my parents and their views on dating. My dad always said I had to wait until I was sixteen. But my mother was absolutely nutty about it. Just hearing me say the word *dating* was enough to make the *chanclas* come flying. The *chanclas* (aka mom's slippers) were soft and fuzzy when they were on her tired feet. However, if one of them was in her right hand, it was as dangerous as a laser-guided missile. The *chancla* was used to keep my brothers and me in line. No matter where we were in the house, if we said or did anything disrespectful, that *chancla* would come flying through the air and smack us. *Swap!* I swore the thing was alive.

"Trust me, I am not going to be baby-talking to anyone anytime soon."

Christie was lying on Sheila's king-size bed, oblivious to the world. The room had floor-to-ceiling windows that looked out over downtown San Jose. Sheila's walls were covered with posters of celebrity hotties. She had a shrine (like mine, but bigger) to Orlando Bloom. There was a life-size cardboard cutout of Legolas right by her bed, piles of romance novels scattered over the floor, and a flat-screen TV with a surround sound stereo system up against the wall. If this had been my room, I wouldn't have minded getting grounded for months.

Christie's strawberry blond hair was tied back in a messy bun with ivory chopsticks. Her gold-colored sandals and freshly manicured toes were dangling off the bed. Christie looked like a totally tanned surfer chick, but she was allergic to sports and anything that involved sweating (except, well, you know). However, she wasn't allergic to athletes. Christie had recently started dating Mark, a beefy blond lacrosse player from our "brother" school, Saint Ignatius. Now she was all goo-goo over him. It was putting a serious strain on our friendship.

I grabbed a fluffy white pillow off Sheila's bed. "I'm going to put a stop to this right now." Christie was ignoring me, whispering who-knows-what into Mark's ear. I couldn't believe what was happening to her. Especially after we'd worked so hard all last year to get her off of academic probation.

Part of my scholarship required me to tutor students after school and over summer vacation. Christie had been my first "tutee." I was really nervous at first because she was the most popular girl at SH. The funny thing was, Christie wasn't stuck-up or conceited in the least. She was the real deal—down-to-earth and friendly. Everyone felt like they knew her and that she was their friend.

The one thing everyone didn't know was that Christie was dyslexic. She tried to hide it by acting as if she couldn't care less about going to college—"Don't worry, I'll just live off my trust fund, Star," she'd say. But I could see the frustration written all over her confused face when she was trying to do her school-work.

After I'd helped Christie pass her English final, she'd taken me under her wing. Until then, I'd been on the fringe of Sacred Heart society, the lone brown girl sitting at the lunch table in the cafeteria, eating my mom's weenie-*con-huevo* burritos by myself. I was constantly worried these girls would eventually get bored with me and move on—kind of like how I'd ditched Tere and Izzy. If that did happen, it probably would serve me right.

Actually, ever since Christie started making out with Mark 24-7, she was already showing signs of being tired of our monthly clothing-swap nights. Once I'd come bearing a couple of thin cotton dresses that *Tía* Lucky had bought at the outlet stores in Gilroy. I could tell Christie was trying to be diplomatic when she'd told me, "These are really pretty, but this look isn't really in right now." I hadn't brought anything after that, so it wasn't technically a swap, because I ended up taking home some of their B-list clothes while they made more room in their closets for the designer threads they bought with their American Express Gold Cards.

Now Christie's idea of "swapping" was trading bodily fluids with Mark. And her grades were slipping because her entire life was revolving around this guy. She needed an intervention, and quick.

"Put the phone down," I said in the same way a cop might tell someone to put down a gun.

"Gimme a minute," Christie answered and pulled a pillow over her face for privacy.

"This is your last warning," I said loudly. Sheila stood holding a pillow on the other side of the bed. I gave Sheila the cue and we both started pounding Christie with our pillows.

"Stop it!" Christie shouted. She wrestled herself up and dashed over to the vanity table on the other side of the room. She and Mark did a quick "I love you more . . . no, I love *you* more . . . no, you . . . no, you!" and then hung up the phone. Christie looked kind of pissed while Sheila laughed uncontrollably.

"You promised!" I said.

"I know, I know." Christie nodded her head in agreement. "But Mark was bored and I couldn't just couldn't let him be lonely."

"Oh please," Sheila groaned. "If he's so lonely, can't he, like, buy a puppy or something?"

"This is supposed to be Swap Night," I reminded her.

A sweet smile appeared on Christie's face. "All right, all right," she said and opened her arms. "Hug?"

We gave in and hugged.

I never knew quite how I felt about Swap Night. On the one hand, it was so much fun to play dress-up with Sheila and Christie. But it wasn't easy to find things that fit my color. Pastels and creamy shades made my dark skin appear yellowish or sickly green, but they made Sheila and Christie's fair complexions glow, which was why their closets were stuffed with lavender and pink everything.

The whole process reminded me how different we were, too—I could never borrow Sheila's makeup, because her foundation was ivory and I needed deep bronze; I could never throw on a pair of Christie's jeans, because she had the flattest butt and mine was large and in charge. Sometimes this seemed like some sort of save-the-poor-kids charity drive and I was essentially the human version of the Salvation Army. It baffled me how being with Sheila and Christie made me feel so adored and ashamed, all at the same time.

"Ooh, Star," Christie said. She held a black ruffled wrap dress up to her chest. "This would look so hot on you."

We were trying on clothes in Sheila's walk-in closet, which was huge. Actually, it was the size of my parent's master bedroom. Both of Sheila's closets were full of all these amazingly nice clothes that my parents would absolutely never have been able to buy for me. A few weeks ago, I'd been trying on one of Christie's new outfits, a very simple slate-blue dress from BCBG. The price tag said $540.00. Just holding the dress in my hand and imagining what my father might think about paying that much for less than a few yards of fabric had made me feel kind of guilty. "*Mija*," he would say. And then he would slowly shake his head. Of course, when I tried it on and saw how amazing it looked, I forgot about all that. At least for a while.

Christie handed me Sheila's black ruffled dress. "Totally try it on. I never wear it anymore." Sheila started pulling out tops and bottoms and building a pile on the floor. "All these things are so old."

I couldn't help but roll my eyes. I thought about what "old" meant in my house. The dress my mother had worn to Tere's *quinceañera* was almost as old as I was.

"I love this!" Christie grabbed a crocheted minidress off a hanger and checked herself out in the mirror. But when she tried it on, she made a disgusted face. "Gross, look at how my fat hangs out on top," she said while pinching her flab. "Sheila, what size do you wear?"

"I'm a two," Sheila bragged.

Christie tugged off the skirt and threw it across the room. "I need to go on a diet. I look like an elephant."

"Shut up," Sheila said to Christie. "An elephant would kill for thighs like yours." Sheila handed me a blue baby-doll dress and I pulled it over my head. It looked ab fab, except for the fact that I didn't have the boobs to hold it up.

"If anyone should be complaining, it should be me. I'm the one with the big butt gene," I joked.

"No, guys like that," Christie stated, as if it were a fact. "Mark is going to dump me when he sees how fat I really am."

"Yeah, you're right," I replied. "Better start starving yourself. And quick!"

"Ha ha," she said. "Oh, hey—I was looking for that necklace." Christie was eyeing the heart-shaped pendant hanging around my neck. She'd lent it to me last month. "I'm sorry, but I'm gonna need it back."

"Sure." I unhooked the delicate white-gold chain dotted with tiny diamonds. It went so perfectly with the black dress I'd worn to Tere's party, and with everything else in my closet. It would have looked especially good with the diamond earrings I had on layaway at Latin Jewelers. After two years of saving my babysitting earnings, I almost had them paid off. I wished I didn't have to give Christie back her necklace. "Thanks again for letting me borrow it."

"No problem. What's mine is yours until I need it again, you know that," Christie said with a wink.

Sheila looked me up and down. "That dress would be so hot to wear on a date. And you can sweep back your hair in a twist, like this." She reached up and pulled my hair back. Then she furrowed her brow and nodded. "Definitely. The guy will love this."

I rolled my eyes. "I'm sure this imaginary guy would love me in this dress on our imaginary date that's never going to happen."

"Speaking of guys," Christie said in a sly, I'm-up-to-something voice, "Sheila, guess who called Mark and asked all about our friend Star?"

"Why, Christie, whoever could it be?" Sheila said overly loudly.

"Kevin McDonough, that really cute guy we saw at the movies last week. The one who looks like Jude Law."

"He's a junior. Plays hoops for Saint Ignatius. So hot," Sheila said, sounding like she was reciting lines she'd rehearsed. "He's into you, Star." She nudged me with her elbow.

"Gee, really?" I said sarcastically.

"Well, obviously it's because he's in awe of your beauty," Christie said with a mischievous grin.

"And don't forget her smokin' booty." Sheila smirked.

"You guys are hysterical," I said.

"So do you want to go out with him?" Christie pressed.

"Yeah, do you, Star? You really should." Sheila nodded emphatically.

"Very funny. I've never even spoken to the guy." I forced a laugh. "Seriously, if Kevin wants to get to know me, you can tell him to send me an e-mail."

"But you never check your account," Sheila moaned.

"'Cause my computer caught a virus," I lied. I didn't even own a computer.

"Star, come on." Sheila sounded serious. "Why do you always do this? Anytime we mention a boy who likes you, you blow him off."

"There are tons of reasons," I replied as I pulled up my jeans. "First of all, my parents have this dumb rule where I can't date. And I know if I tried to hide a boyfriend from them, I'd just get caught. Then I'd get grounded for eternity, and I'd never be able to see you two. I can't bear the thought of life without you, so there." I sat down on Sheila's bed, feeling my weight sink into the fluffy down comforter. I didn't mention the part about how I'd never even kissed a boy before. Or the other part about how before I'd gone to SH, boys had had no interest in me whatsoever and so all this stuff was totally new. And terrifying.

"You're so full of crap!" Sheila shouted and gave me a playful slap on the shoulder. "No one's parents are *that* cruel."

I bit my lower lip. "Well, maybe there is a teeny-tiny chance I could convince them to let me date when I turn fifteen."

"And your birthday is like, in six weeks, right?" Christie asked.

I nodded.

"What are you going to do?"

Images of Tere's tacky *quince* flashed before me. The big puffy dress, the cheesy waltzes, my Nana's dentures mysteriously appearing on top of the cake. No! There was no way I was going to let Sheila and Christie see me like that.

"Probably nothing. Birthdays aren't a big thing in my family."

Sheila looked shocked. "You can't do *nothing*!"

I looked down at my nails and picked at one of my ragged cuticles.

"I know," Christie said. "We'll throw you a party." She jumped up, her face brightening. "And then you can hook up with Kevin."

"And then we can become boyfriend and girlfriend and spend all our time saying smoochy things to each other over the phone," I broke in. *Two parties,* I thought to myself. *I am having two birthday parties.* One for the old Estrella and one for the Estrella I was trying to become.

"Ha ha," Christie said with a giant smile. "This is going to be your best, most important, most amazing life-changing birthday ever!"

My stomach turned with excitement and dread. She had no idea how right she was.

> **barrio** ('bär-ee-o) n., Spanish, slang: 1. neighbor-
> hood or community. For example, the East Side is
> my barrio. 2. The word barrio has a familiar, almost
> enduring feel to it. It's the place we are from—the
> place we call home.

S TEPPING OFF THE BUS AT ALUM ROCK was like stepping into another country. The east side of San Jose was where the Mexicans lived. Not too many white people in these parts, unless they were lost or collecting rent. Abandoned shopping carts lined the sidewalk like white picket fences, local boys chilled on the corners, and the streets were littered with wrappers and trash as if nobody lived here.

But then again, everyone knew each other and looked out for each other. I hadn't even been off the bus for fifteen seconds before I spotted people I knew—*Señora* Gonzalez and *Señora* Ruiz were strolling along, carrying shopping bags. They both waved.

"*Hola*, Estrellíta," *Señora* Gonzalez called out.

"*Hola*," I replied.

Out here, it was like the community was one big crazy family. I crossed the busy intersection, heading toward my house, and my neighborhood welcomed me back.

Ring! Ring! Ring!

The familiar sound of the *paletero* bell carried swiftly through the balmy early-morning air. Rafael Fuentes walked by, dripping with sweat and pushing his fruit Popsicle cart. "*Paletas!*" he called at the top of his lungs. Four neighborhood kids were bouncing around the cart, holding dollar bills in their hands.

Some men I recognized but didn't know by name were cheering as they listened to a soccer match over Spanish radio and ate soft tacos from the corner taco shop. A couple of them nodded hello as I walked by. The delicious aroma of grilled beef and pork lingered around them. LEGOLAND-style homes in mismatched color schemes lined the block. The cracked sidewalks with shards of broken glass contrasted sharply with the pristine, silent streets of Willow Glen.

"Psst! Psst!" a voice whispered, snapping me out of my trance.

I refused to look back. You had to be careful with the boys in the barrio.

"Hey, schoolgirl." The same honeyed voice spoke again as I quickened my pace. "Wait up!"

Gross. Cholo loser, I thought. *If I ignore him, maybe he'll go away.*

"Can I walk you home, Estrella?"

I spun around quickly.

The boy was about my age. He had a shaved head and wore an Aztec warrior T-shirt and dark, baggy jeans. He definitely had this pretty-boy/bad-boy kind of way about him, like a Latino Brad Pitt. There was also a confidence in the way he walked that I recognized. It was that tough-boy exterior that I saw in all the *cholos* in my neighborhood. They drove me crazy! They were always hanging out on the street all day, picking fights, drinking, or getting arrested. But this guy was grinning from ear to ear, like someone with a secret.

"You don't remember me?" he teased and pretended to be hurt.

Those dimples looked familiar. But from where?

"Mrs. Rivera's fourth-grade class," he finally said. "I sat behind you the whole year."

"Agapito?" I asked. Suddenly, I remembered a short, annoying boy with a dark bowl haircut. "Hey! Didn't you once 'accidentally' dump chocolate pudding on my head? And then I chased after you and gave you a bloody nose?"

"That's me! But these days I'm called Speedy." He stood up straighter. "If you tried to chase me now, I'd be able to get away," he said.

"I'm sure I could catch you if I tried," I said. I paused. "But I truly doubt I'd be chasing you now."

"Ouch, baby doll!" he said with a smirk. It seemed like I had impressed him. "You still got that feisty tongue. Haven't changed much, huh?"

Well, I knew one thing hadn't changed: we'd only been talking for ten seconds and I already had an urge to punch him in the nose again. But he sure had grown these last couple of years. He almost looked like a man. If he hadn't been so annoying, he'd actually have been really cute.

My face grew hot with embarrassment and I quickly turned toward home.

"Do you always walk this fast, or do you have to pee?" he asked, laughing at his own joke.

"No one asked you to walk with me, so why don't you just take off?" I hurried around the corner.

"Maybe tomorrow, Estrellíta, you'll be in a better mood!" I heard him shout.

What the hell had happened? Agapito Padilla? It had been years since I'd seen him. He'd obviously turned into a *cholo*. The shaved head and baggy pants gave him away. That meant he was just like all the other thugs in the barrio. Not a week went by in my house when my parents didn't mention Marta and what had happened to her when she'd gotten mixed up with those losers. Poor Marta. I felt a tightness in my chest when I thought about her.

My small yellow house sat in the middle of the block, with stumps in front where great big palm trees once stood. The wide street was usually lined with broken-down cars and just then, some little boys were outside playing football. The ball flew right behind me, so I picked it up and tossed it to seven-year-old Diego Lopez.

He gave me a gap-toothed grin. "Thank you, 'strella!"

Diego lived a block away in a house almost identical to ours, but his was bright orange. In fact, all of our neighbors had similar one-story cottagelike homes, which were painted in gaudy carnival colors and draped in festive holiday decorations that never came down. (For instance, the Montoyas, who lived three houses to the right, kept a Nativity scene up all year long.)

My house leaned to the left like it was trying to pull itself from the roots and run away. The front lawn was full of weed patches, a few white chairs, and car oil stains. Bobby and Rey were out front working on Bobby's silver '99 Honda Civic.

Bobby and Rey fit in well wherever they went because they were average guys' guys. All they ever talked about was sports, and they never had any serious girlfriends. Bobby had worked for two straight years bagging groceries so he could buy his car last summer. They spent most weekend nights cruising around downtown San Jose, "looking for action," which of course they never found.

Now Rey was installing new chrome rims on the car. Bobby was jumpy. He was trying to make sure his favorite Sharks T-shirt and backwards baseball hat didn't get all dirty. Rey's brow was all bunched together as he handled a socket wrench. He had just gotten his haircut, a close fade, which was popular among his girlfriendless buddies. Some *chica* once lied to him and said he was dreamy. He never forgot it and walked around with airs of *macho* grandeur. The radio blasted WILD 94.9, a hip-hop and freestyle station. They were nodding to the bass.

"Hey, guys. What's up?" I asked.

"Estrella," Bobby said. A huge toothy smile suddenly graced his wide face as he took me into a bear hug and picked me up off the ground. "What's up, Shorty?"

I pointed to the rims and admired them. "Those are tight."

Rey got up, cleaned off his hands on his jeans, and smiled. "I picked these up from this guy in the city. All the ladies are gonna be beggin' to get a ride on these wheels."

"That's right!" Bobby shouted and gave Rey a high five.

"Have you guys seen Mom?" I asked.

"Yeah," Bobby said, grinning. "She kicked us out about an hour ago. Looks like she's got some top-secret business in store for you." He chuckled some more and then jabbed Rey in the ribs.

"What's going on?" I asked Bobby. "Come on, tell me!"

I began to flex my fingers and crack my knuckles. Bobby was a big guy. He intimidated many people. His nickname was Grizzly, which made sense because he had my father's wide frame and hefty appetite. But the boy was deathly afraid of a good tickle. He was putty in my bony hands.

Bobby put up his arms in defense. "Hey, don't even go there, sis."

"Then tell me what they're up to and I'll back off."

Before Bobby could respond, Rey grabbed my arms, pinned them behind me, and said in a pirate voice, "Har, me matey. Let's show her how we deal with unruly wenches!"

Bobby went on the offensive and started to tickle me. I tried to kick him with my free leg, but he grabbed ahold of both of them, and he and Rey began to swing me from side to side in the air.

Suddenly, my mother appeared by the door. "What are you bullies doing?" she shouted. She was wearing her typical house clothes—slippers and the ruffled checkered apron that she'd bought at a church bazaar. She frowned as she marched down the steps. "Put your sister down right now!"

"Ah, come on, Mom," Bobby whined. "She started it! We're just having a little fun."

"Estrella's not a little girl anymore," she scolded them, while taking her *chancla* off her foot. Then she gave me a disapproving look. Upon seeing the infamous slipper in her hand, the boys put me down immediately.

Rey turned around his baseball hat. "Come on, man. Let's go downtown."

"Hey, I want to go, too," I pleaded.

"Estrella Maria Serena Alvarez! Come inside right now, young lady!" my mother ordered, with the *chancla* still in her hand.

"But Mom!"

"No buts. Inside!"

"Have fun." Rey snickered and stuck out his tongue. He and Bobby were still laughing as they got into the car and started the engine.

Sulking, I followed my mom into the house.

When my mother wasn't teaching at Head Start, she was collecting rare junk and forgettable memorabilia. She spent her weekends haggling with shifty-eyed vendors at the San Jose flea market over twenty-five cents. As a kid, I loved to go "hunting for treasure" with her, but now it was just too embarrassing. Mom always had big plans—to fix the leg of an antique coffee table, mend a Victorian quilt, or reupholster a chair she'd found on the street corner. But she rarely got around to any of these projects. The living room had become a way station for all her finds, along with the dozens of family portraits, awards, and religious icons (gifts from my nana) that competed for space on the cluttered cream-colored walls.

My aunt Lucrecia (aka *Tía* Lucky) was hunched over the DVD player. Her flat butt was covered in leopard-print spandex pants. *Tía* Lucky was our family's Avon representative. Whenever we had an event to go to—like Tere's *quinceañera* the day before—she insisted on covering me and my mother with about ten pounds of makeup. Each. She talked about Spanish soap stars like they were her personal friends, and she liked to shop at Forever 21 because it made her feel young. Although my *tía* had a curvy figure, half-cut tees with spandex shorts didn't do her any justice. She'd had a beauty mark tattooed right near her mouth, and pencil-thin eyebrows that were just a tad too high on her forehead. She always looked a little shocked.

"*A ver, a ver, a ver,*" she repeated while fidgeting with the controls.

"Estrellíta!" My mother waved excitedly. "We were just talking about how beautiful you looked yesterday. Come sit next to me."

She scooted over on the green plastic-covered couch and took my hand. Her touch was warm and soft. It reminded me of when I was a little girl—she would caress my head while singing me to sleep. *She hasn't done that in a long time,* I thought as I looked at the dark crescent moons underlining her brown eyes.

"I have something for you, *mija*," she said with a mischievous smile. And with that, she removed a tiny black box from her apron and handed it to me as if it were the Holy Grail. It said LATIN JEWELERS on it in small gold letters.

I opened it, and inside was a giant, gaudy-looking gold-colored ring with the number fifteen in the middle of it.

"I know it is a little bit early to be giving you this, but I saw it on sale downtown and I knew you needed to have it. It's a traditional *quinceañera* ring. Go ahead, put it on." She nodded encouragingly.

Slowly, I took the ring out of the box. I prayed it would be too small as I slipped it on the ring finger of my right hand. No luck—a perfect fit.

My mother grabbed my hand so she could admire the ring. It was too chunky, and the color was off, so it was more yellow than golden. I thought about the beautiful delicate necklace I'd given back to Christie, how much I loved that and how much I hated this. Then I looked back up at my mother's face.

"Do you like it?" Her eyes were bright. "Ever since you were born I've dreamed of the day I'd give you your *quinceañera* ring."

I tried to force a smile and swallowed hard. "Thanks, Mom."

"I knew you'd like it." My mother held my gaze for a moment until my *tía* started yelling at the TV.

"Eh, come on! What's wrong with you? You never work!"

"Look! Look!" my mother cried. The TV lit up in fuzzy, barely viewable images. *"Mira,* there she is. Do you see your cousin?"

Tía Lucky perched on the brown La-Z-Boy but seemed unsure whether the dilapidated chair would hold her weight. It was one of Mom's projects, so it was held together with rope and coat hanger wire for extra support. *Tía* Lucky was chewing loudly on a stick of gum. "Isn't she beautiful?"

"Look at her dress!" my mother said, patting my leg as if I hadn't seen the dress countless times before.

Tía Lucky smiled. "We got that dress in Tijuana. It cost me two hundred bucks. You can't get that quality anymore," she continued in a haughty voice. The woman who made it, *está* . . ." She started pinching the air with her fingers, like she was going to find the words in the sky. "What was her name? Anyway, she died last year. And she learned from her mother, who learned from *her* mother." *Tía* shook her head. "Such a shame Marta only wore it once. It's just sitting there in the closet, collecting dust." It was so strange to see *Tía* watching Marta on the television with such love in her eyes. Yesterday she had barely glanced at her daughter.

In our family, tradition was everything. Nana never let us forget all the sacrifices she'd made to bring us here. As a kid, I would get nightmares when she'd tell me about how she'd crossed the Rio Grande with two kids strapped to her back and five pesos clenched in her teeth. She'd been eighteen, with only a third-grade education, and had spoken no English. Now she owned her own house, could read the Bible (in English and Spanish), and had great dentures. Nana wouldn't let us forget that none of this could have been possible in San Idelfonso, the small rural town in northern Mexico where our family came from.

My mother and *tía* had never gotten to have their own *quinces,* so all their hopes fell on the next generation's shoulders.

My *tía* had tried to give Marta everything a young girl could desire, including a fancy *quinceañera*, which I knew she was still paying for. At the time, it had made sense for Marta to have a *quinceañera*. Marta was born in Mexico and that was what they did over there. I was born in San Jose, California. None of my school friends had had *quinceañeras*. Marta was Mexican; I was an American. That was a big difference.

"Uh, Mom . . ." I hesitated. "I really should be studying right now."

My mother tucked a lock of my hair behind my ear and smiled. "You can study later."

"Mom," I started again. "Aren't you the one who's always saying how important school is and how I have to study really hard if I'm ever going to make something of myself?"

"Come on, Estrella," my mother teased. "Live a little. There's more to life than schoolwork."

The TV zoomed in on my cousin's robust backside. She was waltzing around the dance floor with her sleepy-eyed male partner.

"You are going to look so beautiful," said my mother. "I can barely wait."

cholo ('cho-low) n., Spanish, informal: 1. a style sub-
set among Mexican-American urban youth. Cholos
sometimes have tattoos of names or pictures of the
Virgin Mary on their bodies, and shaved heads. They
like to wear long-sleeve flannel shirts, khaki pants, and
drive lowriders. 2. chola: a female who likes to hang
out with cholos. Wears hoochie-mama clothes and
has lots of makeup, penciled-in eyebrows, and big hair
3. Cholo is also a term used to describe a gangster.

THE NEXT MORNING, I WALKED INTO THE KITCHEN to find
my mother singing off-key with the chorus to Vicente
Fernández's "El Rey" while scrambling eggs and *chorizo* in a
cast-iron pan. *I can't believe how happy organizing this silly party
makes her,* I thought. But it was nice to see her smile.

"*Mija,*" she called out while wiping her hands on her apron,
"hurry up. You're late."

Still half asleep, I shuffled to the bathroom. Bobby and Rey were snoring loudly in their room. They were so lucky. Their school was just a couple of blocks away, so they never had to wake up before the sun.

As the bathroom filled up with hot steam and I shampooed my hair, my mother yelled from the other side of the door.

"*Mija*, I need you to come straight home from school. While you were studying last night, your *tía* and I agreed that she'd bring the dress over this afternoon."

"What dress?" I asked as I tried to get soap out of my eyes. The door opened and all the heat escaped out of the bathroom.

"Marta's *quince* dress, silly. It just needs to be fitted. It'll be perfect."

"Mom, I don't know. . . . I'm just not sure it's *me*."

"Nonsense. It'll look beautiful on you. You'll see," she said before shutting the door.

Marta's dress was the most hideous thing I'd ever seen. It was made of shiny neon-orange satinlike (satin*like*) fabric and covered in ruffles. Marta had looked like an orange layer cake. God was definitely punishing me for something.

"For whatever I did, I'm sorry!" I said while looking up at the ceiling, and a feeling of impeding doom loomed over me.

I was so late that I rushed out of the house without blow-drying my hair. The back of my shirt was soaking wet, but I didn't mind. Actually, it was cooling me off on this warm early morning. My neighborhood was already bustling with activity. *Señora* Gamboa was racing down the street to catch the bus,

Rafael Fuentes was pushing his *paletas* cart, and little Diego Lopez was sitting in the middle of his driveway poking a rock with a stick.

"Psst! Psst!" came a voice from behind me. I turned around. Oh no. "Are you stalking me?" I said.

"Stalking? Nah, I'm just going to school." Speedy smiled and held up a new spiral-bound notebook as proof.

"School? Yeah, right." I laughed and continued walking toward the bus stop around the corner.

"Wait a second, I have something for you," he said. Then, like a magician performing a trick, he pulled out a yellow rose from behind his back. He had obviously picked it from someone's yard. The flower had wilted a little, and its thorns were poking out.

"What's this?"

He stood there, holding the flower steady. "It's a peace offering."

"For what?" I asked suspiciously. *What did he want?*

He shrugged and gave me a crooked smile. "I know I used to bug you all the time when we were kids. I can think of five separate occasions when I dumped my dessert on your head. But that was then. I want us to be friends now."

"Friends?" I'd never been given a flower before. But something about the self-confident smirk on his face told me not to trust this boy.

"Yo, Speedy," a rock-hard *cholo* with a shaved head and dark glasses called out from across the street. "C'mere, man."

"I'll be right back," Speedy said to me before dashing over to him. The *cholo* whispered something into his ear.

"Figures," I sighed, shoving the rose into my backpack pocket. *Probably dealing drugs,* I thought as I continued down the street without him.

"Yo!" Speedy shouted and ran to catch up with me. "I told you I'd just be a minute, *fresita*."

"Some of us don't have all day to hang in the street," I said, quickening my pace. "And I'm not a *fresa*."

"Oh no?" He smiled. "I see you walking around with your nose in the air, like you're too good or something. But that's okay. I like my women feisty."

"I'll show you feisty!" I snapped. He'd gone too far. So I punched him in the nose, just like I had back in Mrs. Rivera's class. I really hadn't planned to hit him, nor did I use all my strength. However, Speedy turned at the same time and hit my fist. His face went pale from shock and he stumbled backwards.

"I'm so sorry," I said. "I didn't mean to hit you so hard." His nose was bleeding a little. Jesus, what had come over me?

"Damn, girl." He smirked. "Two bloody noses in less than ten years! I'll never call you that again."

I gave him some tissue. "Are you okay?"

"Yeah, sure."

I checked my watch. "Oh my God, I'm going to be so late."

"Hey, let me help you with your books," he said while taking my bag. "They look heavy."

We were standing at the corner when something whooshed by us.

"That's my bus!" I screamed, following it with my index finger as it sped down the avenue.

"Hurry, maybe we can catch it!" he yelled as he sprinted ahead of me. I watched his feet pound the pavement at a lightning pace, and, incredibly, he made it to the next bus stop before the last passenger got on. I jogged behind him, my wet ponytail swinging to and fro. Thankfully, the bus driver waited.

"I guess I'm lucky they call you Speedy. Thank you." I said as we boarded.

"Don't worry about it—it's nothing."

The aisle was packed with early-morning commuters. We made our way to the back and held on tight to the pole as the bus raced through traffic.

"You know, my school's very far away," I said.

"That's all right. I've got time," he said with a grin. He had the most contagious smile. I couldn't help but smile back.

Then there was an awkward silence between us. I could tell he was nervous. He kept wiping his brow, even though there was no sweat on it. *Was I making him nervous?* I wondered. When our eyes locked, my body got really stiff. It didn't make sense. This was *Agapito*, the boy who used to tie my shoelaces together. He was always getting in trouble for playing paper football during math class. But that was a long time ago, and Speedy was all grown up now.

"Hey," I said, "who was that *cholo*? Friend of yours?"

"You mean Lobo? He's cool."

Lobo, I thought. That nickname fit him well. He looked dangerous, like he would have no problem removing a person's head with his teeth. "What did he want?"

"Nothing."

"It seemed important."

"It was nothing."

"Didn't look like nothing."

"What's your problem? I told you it was nothing, okay? Leave it alone." His eyes became cold.

How rude. "Well, if that's what you call friendship, then I don't think I care for it." I rolled my eyes and turned to look out the window.

"Stop with the attitude, okay?" he replied. I continued to ignore him and looked at my watch as if he were wasting my time.

"All right," he finally said.

I shrugged encouraging him to go on.

"Well . . ." Whatever it was it was making him squirm. His lips were pressed together hard. But I just stared at him, waiting.

"It's kind of a business thing we have."

"I knew it!" I said loud enough for the entire bus to hear. "You're dealing drugs."

Speedy's mouth dropped and he gasped like he'd been sucker-punched in the stomach. His shocked expression made me wonder if maybe I'd guessed wrong.

The entire bus stopped talking and stared at Speedy. An old woman with blue hair and a bleached mustache said, "Shame on you, *mijo*. You're too young for that life."

"*Señora*," Speedy said seriously, "you got it all wrong. I don't deal drugs. I don't do drugs. I don't even drink," he pleaded as if the crowd on the bus was a jury. "I sell clothes."

I was too stunned to react.

The woman looked into his eyes and said, "Then why do you dress like a *cholo?*"

Speedy's cheeks turned bright red.

I felt horrible. *Speedy must think I'm a terribly judgmental person,* I thought to myself. *But that's not me.* I dodged his eyes and headed for the door.

"Estrella!" Speedy called out after me.

I pushed the guy in front of me aside and hurried off the bus. Speedy jumped off right after me.

"This isn't your school, is it, *fresita?*" he said.

Why was he following me? Didn't he see what a jerk I'd become? "Leave me alone," I mumbled. The bus took off, leaving us alone on the street.

"Why are you so wound up, girl? I'm the one who should be mad."

I was about to say something, but he was right. I snapped my mouth shut.

"Okay," he said, misunderstanding my silence. "It seems like you don't need anybody, so I'm going to leave you alone."

Speedy began strolling across the street. *Good riddance,* I thought. It was only then that I realized I was in the seedy industrial part of downtown. It smelled like a men's urinal. Abandoned graffiti-covered buildings were boarded up with FOR SALE signs on the front doors. Day laborers stood on the corners waving down potential customers. Other men argued on cell phones or were sleeping off hangovers on the sidewalk. It was definitely not a good thing to be in my school uniform and standing on a street corner alone.

And if that wasn't bad enough, Marshall & Sons, the roofing company where my dad worked, was just down the block. Dad always took this route to work. He'd be so pissed if he caught me here. *But dad's never up at this time*, I thought. He wasn't a morning person and started work at eleven. Either way, I was going to have to swallow my pride and ask Speedy to wait with me for the next bus.

"Hold on, Speedy," I called out. But he just kept on walking. "Speedy! Come back!"

He turned around this time. He put both his hands on his hips and raised his eyebrows at me.

"I'll come back, but only if you apologize for announcing to the entire bus that I was a drug dealer."

"I didn't call you a drug dealer. I just said you sold drugs!" I tried to smile, but he didn't smile back.

"If you want me to be your friend, you'll have to apologize."

I let out a sigh. "Fine! I'm sorry."

And with that, Speedy trotted back toward me. His face was about three feet away from mine when he gave me another grin. "Now, that wasn't so hard, was it?"

"No," I said, trying to hide my smile. I looked at my watch. Damn, I was going to be late again. "You sure you don't mind waiting with me until the next bus comes?"

"I don't mind at all," he said. "In fact, I'm glad you got off the bus. This way we can catch up."

I was unsure of where to begin. "So, you sell clothes?"

"Yeah," Speedy replied.

"When we were little, you used to sell candy at school," I said. "Always the little businessman, huh?"

"I guess so. Remember how I always had to shove those chili-flavored lollipops into my bag when Mrs. Rivera walked by? Well, it's sort of like that now, too. You see, Lobo has a cousin who works for this major clothing line. So his cousin hooks us up with boxes and we sell them. Easy money." He smiled proudly. "On the down low."

"But aren't those clothes stolen?"

"We like to say that we're *liberating* the clothes."

"Huh?"

"Estrella, check it out—clothes are a major industry. Most of the big clothing companies have big factories all over Latin America. Those companies pay their workers pennies to make the clothes we buy in the U.S. for hundreds of dollars. These companies are getting fat on swindling our people."

"You're still stealing." I didn't really know about the factories, but selling stolen clothes just felt wrong to me.

"So are they," Speedy answered. "They're stealing from us. Those clothes are worth a couple of dollars, but they sell them at five and ten times what they're worth, because they can."

"You think you're some type of Robin Hood."

Speedy smirked. "Totally, but you can call me Speedy from the hood." He started to laugh. I couldn't help but laugh, too.

Suddenly, the sound of a mufflerless pickup caught my attention. It was a familiar-looking 1970s rusty red El Camino. My father loved his truck, which was a dinosaur from his cruisin' days, and refused to get a new one. He said it brought him good luck. Maybe it did, but his luck was gonna get me in deep trouble.

I had no time to think, so I just reacted. I hurled myself behind the biggest thing I could find—a Dumpster.

Speedy was completely confused. "What are you doing?"

"Shh!" I pressed my index finger to my lips. "Be very, very quiet!"

My heart began to palpitate as the sound of the coughing motor came to a stop. A chill swept over my body as I heard the familiar creak of the car door opening.

"What's wrong?" Speedy was obviously unaware of my imminent doom. Dad was always warning me about talking to boys in the neighborhood. Bobby and Rey were never allowed to hang out in the streets. They'd been shoved into athletics and automania at an early age to keep them busy. There was no way my father would approve of Speedy and me hanging out.

All of a sudden, a huge dark shadow hovered over me. Normally my dad was a friendly looking man. He had thick wavy black hair sprinkled with light patches of gray. He smiled a lot, and his top lip was covered with a thick, furry mustache. He had a beer belly that drooped over his belt buckle, a husky frame, and sun-bronzed skin from working outdoors all day. My dad was only about five foot six, but when he was angry, like he was now, he managed to make himself look about ten feet tall.

"I *thought* that was you," Dad said, looking down at me.

I smiled and nervously straightened my skirt. "I missed my bus. Can I get a ride?"

"Who's this?" He checked out Speedy, taking note of the red bandanna hanging from his back pocket and what I knew he would call a "slick hoodlum" demeanor. My father had a strange expression on his face, like he was eating something really disgusting.

"This is Agapito." I gulped. *I'm dead.* "We were in fourth grade in Mrs. Rivera's class together."

My words didn't seem to make him less angry. "What are you doing? Playing hooky with this boy? Get in the truck now!" he shouted and reached out for me. Quickly, I darted around him and hopped into the passenger seat. As Dad was walking around the front of the car, Speedy leaned over to me and whispered real quick, "I'd love to take you out sometime and—"

But then Dad got in the car and slammed the door shut behind him. He stomped down on the gas pedal, leaving Speedy in a storm of exhaust and smoke.

For the next five minutes, there was nothing but an unsettling silence, except for when we hit traffic and Dad started cursing to himself in Spanish. That was a bad sign, because he only did that when he was about to rip into someone.

The tension in the air was killing me. "Dad, I want to explain—"

"Explain what?" he shouted. He was gripping the steering wheel so tightly, his knuckles were white. "You think I'm stupid!"

"No, it's just that—"

"Estrella, were you or were you not downtown when you're supposed to be at school?"

"I was, but—"

"But nothing," he fumed. "I'm not going to sit back and let you throw your life away. But I'm late. I don't have time for your stupid games."

I glared out the window. There was no talking to Dad. He seemed to think that if he didn't watch me every second, I would end up either pregnant or involved in gangs and not graduate from high school. This was the worst thing he could possibly imagine. My dad had always wanted to go to college, and I'd once heard him mention a math scholarship he'd won in high school. But when Mom got pregnant with my brothers, he had to start working. With Marta following in his footsteps and my brothers failing everything but football, I was the one he was counting on.

After about twenty minutes, the car came to an abrupt stop in front of my school.

"I want to talk to you when you get home. You hear me?" he grunted.

"*Sí, papá*," I said and dashed out as I heard the bell for first period ring.

mensa ('men-sa) n., Spanish, informal: 1. It means stupid or dumb in English. My brothers like to call me mensa as if it were my middle name. That's why they're dorks. 2. It can also be used affectionately when you do or say something silly.

AFTER THAT, THINGS ONLY GOT WORSE. I'd gone as fast as I could—sprinted all the way across the giant bright green lawn, up the stairs that led to the huge mahogany doors, and flown down the enormous hallway to my classroom—but I'd still been five minutes late. So Sister Mary Elena (I called her Mister because I was convinced she used to be a man—women don't have Adam's apples, do they?) had given me my third tardy slip in four days, which meant I'd be stuck in after-school detention.

Then Mr. Peterson had caught me passing notes with Sheila in social studies, so he sent me to "Hobo Row"—this line of desks that faced the wall, where all the "delinquents" sat. Of course, the delinquents at SH—a bunch of pretty white girls with blond hair tucked behind their diamond-studded ears—looked like a bunch of Girl Scouts compared to the *cholas* in my neighborhood.

Fortunately, I'd made it through the first half of the day in one piece, and now it was lunchtime and I could enjoy hanging out with my girls. I met up with them at the front door of SH. Sheila was leaning against one of the ultramodern chrome lockers, applying another coat of her signature bloodred lipstick that always made the nuns wonder about the state of her "virtue." That chick loved to cause controversy and attract attention. A few days ago, Sister Regis had caught her smoking in the girls' bathroom, and instead of putting her cigarette out like she was ordered to, Sheila had blown a puff right into Sister Regis's face. I'd be seeing her later at detention for sure.

Christie was sitting cross-legged on the shiny wooden stairs, fiddling with her hair, which was held back with a simple black satin ribbon. Last month, she'd watched *Breakfast at Tiffany's* with her mom, and since then she'd been obsessed with Audrey Hepburn, which didn't surprise me—Christie was always obsessed with something. A few months ago, she'd insisted on straightening my coarse, frumpy hair with a hot iron and giving me blond highlights because she thought it would make me look like Carmen Electra. After weeks of nagging, I'd finally let her. The result: a nice blend of Carmen Electra and the Bride of Frankenstein. We'd taken a midnight trip to the drugstore for a box of hair color and dyed it back later that night. But even to this day, she was still apologizing.

"So what are we doing for eats?" I asked as we started the five-block walk to the mini–outdoor shopping center. That's where a lot of the girls from Sacred Heart went for lunch. The U, as it was commonly called, was an assortment of chain restaurants like Burger King and Taco Bell assembled in a half circle. It also had some small specialty restaurants and boutique shops where we liked to chill when school was over.

Sheila and Christie gave each other knowing glances.

Christie and Sheila loved to eat out for lunch, but it always made me edgy because it was expensive. Five dollars here, ten there. It really added up at the end of the week. Sheila or Christie would usually treat me, and that just made me feel like a beggar.

"Well," Christie said, "I noticed how depressed you were in English and thought you needed a pick-me-up." She had just changed into her new high-heeled ankle boots. They were totally against the dress code. Christie used to get busted all the time, so she'd started carrying them in her book bag. That way, she could change as soon as she walked off school property.

"We figured you needed to talk," Sheila added. "And you know how nosy everyone is at school."

I nodded. They were my friends, and friends tell each other when something is wrong. So why did the idea of confiding in them just make me feel *more* anxious?

"So hey," Christie said as we walked. "My parents gave me their credit card to go shopping over the weekend and then this morning when I tried to give it back, my dad just shook his head and said something about treating my friends to lunch. Looks like it's on me today!"

Christie was so generous, but it was easy for her because she had so much. Her folks were hella cool. They trusted her so much and even let her stay alone when they left town for the weekend. I was never allowed anywhere by myself. It had taken me an entire year to convince my parents that it was okay for me to take the city bus to school. Sheila had it good, too. Her mom was like her best friend. When Sheila told her mom she was dating a few different guys because she wasn't sure who she liked the best, her mom just said, "That's what being young is for!" And then she gave her a big box of condoms! If I'd even *said* the word *condoms* to my mother, her head would probably have popped right off.

We stopped in front of a hole-in-the-wall restaurant with cool bamboo benches on the patio and purple orchids on the windowsill. The sign above the door said MOSHI MOSHI.

"You guys up for sushi?" Christie asked.

"Whatever Star wants," Sheila said.

I casually checked the menu on the window. *Maki maki? Wakame? Ugh,* I thought. I had no idea what any of these things were, but thankfully there were pictures. "Sounds good to me," I said with a smile.

Sheila nodded and we sat down at a small round table by the door.

"Hey, Sheila, didn't your mom just get back from Tokyo?" I asked.

"Yeah," Sheila said. "She brought me back the cutest kimono. You should see it. It's gorgeous."

"I bet," I responded as I looked around the restaurant. The room was decorated with mini flags and pictures of sumo wrestlers. "Why don't you order for us? I always just end up getting the same thing when I have sushi, y'know?"

Sheila took a lunch menu from the waiter. "Sure. By the way, this place has great shiromi usuzukuri."

"Okay. Yeah, I've always wanted to try that."

Part of me loved the fact that my friends were so worldly, but sometimes when I was with them, I felt like a little kid. I was used to being the smart one in the family—the one who helped my mom balance her checkbook or program the DVD player. It frustrated me to admit that I didn't know something. And whenever I was with Sheila and Christie, I found myself struggling to keep up.

The waiter brought some tea, cloth napkins, and chopsticks wrapped in white paper. Christie ripped open the wrapper and split the wood in two. She then rubbed the chopsticks together like she was trying to start a fire.

"So, what's up?" Sheila poured hot tea into our cups.

I tried to copy Christie in hopes that they wouldn't notice my total lack of coordination with chopsticks. "My dad's on my case again." I said. "He's all pissed off just because I missed the bus. Whatever."

Sheila sipped her tea as she listened, nodding her head every now and then.

"Because you missed the bus?" Christie snorted. "Wow, that's retarded." She reached over to grab her cup and dropped her chopsticks on the floor. "Oops," she smiled. Christie raised her hand and called out, "Waiter!"

Well, maybe I could tell them what happened, I thought. After all, they were my best friends. "It's just not fair," I began. "I'm supposed to be a good girl, follow his rules, and not give him any trouble. But my brothers get away with murder. When they were my age, they didn't even have a curfew! They can do anything they want because they're guys. It's stupid macho crap."

"Men are scum," Sheila said. A tired-looking waiter with a receding hairline brought Christie another set of chopsticks. Then Sheila turned to the waiter and said a whole bunch of words, none of which I understood. I could only guess that she must have been ordering our lunch.

"So? I don't get it," Christie asked. "Your dad got pissed because you missed the bus when your brothers miss the bus all the time?"

"Well, not exactly." I took a sip of burning-hot tea.

They waited for me to go on.

"He found me with a boy."

"So that's what this is about!" Sheila slapped the table. "Yeah! I knew it had to be something juicy."

"You and a guy? I don't believe this!" Christie shouted loud enough for the Mexican cooks in the back to hear. "Details. I need details, woman! I don't believe it. Here I've been bending over backwards to hook you up with Kevin—"

"And you're already getting it on at the bus stop!" Sheila broke in.

"Well," I sighed, looking down at my little ceramic cup of tea, "it's nothing like that." My hands started to sweat.

"Did you kiss him?" Sheila asked. The couple next to us

turned in annoyance, but Sheila and Christie didn't notice or seem to care.

"What does he look like?" Christie said

"When can we meet him?" Sheila pressed.

"Ladies," I said, "calm down. It's not what you think." The couple turned around again and I smiled in embarrassment.

"Then tell us!"

"Shhh!" *We're going to get thrown out,* I thought. "He's this guy from my neighborhood."

Sheila and Christie nodded. Was I imagining it, or did Christie furrow her eyebrows slightly when I said *my neighborhood?*

"I went to elementary school with him. He used to be this little brat, but he's turned into a totally hot guy. He looks just like Oscar de la Hoya."

"Oscar who?" They looked confused.

"Like Enrique Iglesias," I said, trying to come up with another Latin boy they would recognize. It wasn't a total exaggeration. I was sure that if Enrique shaved his head, got a tan, and dressed like a cholo, he would've looked just like Speedy.

Christie smirked. "Whatever. Spanish guys are hot."

I couldn't believe that they didn't know who Oscar de la Hoya was. He was only the finest Mexican-American to ever win a gold medal at the Olympics. *Tere and Izzy would have recognized him,* I thought.

"And?" Sheila asked impatiently. She wanted the whole story.

"And I missed my bus and he waited with me."

Sheila gave me a sideways glance. "Waited with you. You mean he doesn't have a car?"

"Well, I don't know."

"Don't even bother," Christie said, dismissing him with the wave of her hand. "I once dated this guy without a car." She made a disgusted face. "He had his parents drive us around in their Land Rover. It was so embarrassing. His folks actually went along with us on the date. They sat a couple of rows behind us at the theater. He tried to put his arm around me and his mom let out this big, loud, obviously fake cough to let him know to cut it out. It was terrible. I never saw him again."

I felt my face turning red.

Sheila crinkled her nose and shook her head in disapproval. "Yeah, Star, you deserve better."

Christie took out her cell phone. "In fact, why don't we call Kevin right now?"

"What?" I suddenly felt nauseous. It seemed a little weird that they were dismissing Speedy so quickly. It was like they hadn't even heard anything I was saying. "But I don't want to call Kevin."

"It's not a big deal," Sheila said.

"Maybe he and Mark can meet us. They're always together anyway," Christie suggested as she dialed.

"Wait, guys," I said. I shook my head no, but it was too late.

"Sweetheart!" Christie cried into the phone. "Listen, what are you guys doin'? I got Star here and she wants to talk to Kevin. What do you mean? C'mon, just for a second. She really wants to talk to him." She looked up at me and winked.

Christie passed me her phone. I just stared at it like I didn't know how to use it. Sheila jabbed me in the rib.

"Hello?" I said.

"Hey!"

"Kevin?"

"Yeah, what's going on, girl?" he asked.

Both Sheila and Christie were looking at me expectantly and nodding.

"I'm good," I said, my voice trembling a little. "Um, I mean, I'm having lunch with Sheila and Christie."

"Sweet. Listen, I can't talk much; I'm getting ready for practice. But can I call you later?" he asked.

"Sure," I said.

"What's your number?"

All of a sudden, I went into panic mode. Kevin couldn't call my house. My parents would freak. Or totally embarrass me in front of him. Or both.

"Why don't you give me yours and I'll call you?"

As if on cue, Sheila handed me a pen.

I took down his number on my napkin and turned off the phone.

"Fabulous," Christie said. "Good job. I'm proud of you."

But it just didn't feel right.

"Star, you don't look happy. Did Kevin say something?" Sheila asked.

"No, it's not that." I tried to smile. "He was cool. I was just thinking about all the crap I'm going to hear when I get home."

"Well, I know what'll make you feel better," Sheila said, giving Christie a nod.

"Yeah," Christie said. "My folks are going to Tahoe at the end of the month. They said it was okay if I had your birthday party at my house while they're gone."

"Oh my God!" I said. "I didn't realize you were so serious! That's so tight."

"We'll invite only extremely hot guys," Sheila said.

"For sure," Christie and I agreed.

"I could get a bunch of CDs from my brothers," I suggested.

"Just have them e-mail me some MP3s; then we can figure out a playlist," Christie said.

"Right, but actually maybe your music would be better," I said quickly. "They're all into Korn now and Black Sabbath and whatever."

"And I'll make sure Kevin McDonough is there." Christie smiled coyly.

"Don't you ever stop?" I said.

"Not when it comes to you, Star," Sheila said. "Besides, I think you and Kevin would make a much better couple than you and some random guy who doesn't even have a car."

"Me too," Christie said as our food arrived.

Two square plates with thinly sliced burritolike rolls of rice appeared in the center of the table. They were garnished with a green paste and little pieces of something pink. I stared at the food.

"So what am I going to wear?" Sheila asked. "I think I'll need to get something new."

"Sheila, you have, like, a hundred outfits," I teased.

"Yeah, but you've seen me in all of them." Sheila plucked a piece of sushi off the dish with her chopsticks and popped it into her mouth.

"Hey, what's that?" Sheila said, pointing to my giant yellow *quinceañera* ring. *Crap*, I'd forgotten I was still wearing it. "Sporting some new *bling*, I see?" Sheila smirked.

"Oh, ha! No, this is nothing," I put my hand under the table. "Just something my mom gave me." I blushed.

"Well, that was nice of her. But does your *mom* think you're a rapper?" Christie teased.

I looked up at Christie's hands. She had short, rounded nails, a perfect French manicure, and a thin gold ring with three tiny little rubies sparkling on the middle finger of her right hand.

"Yeah. Ha, ha. It's just sort of . . . a family thing. Like an inside joke," I said.

"Hmmm," Sheila said. I put my hands under the table and twisted the ring around so that only the back of the band was showing. I looked down at my hands in my lap—still ugly, but a little better.

"Why don't we head over to Santana Row after school?" I said quickly, trying to change the subject. "It'll be fun."

I attempted to grab a piece of the seaweed concoction, but it fell off my chopsticks and landed on the floor.

"Need some help?" The waiter appeared with a fork.

I smiled, feeling *mensa*. My face turned red as I took the fork.

"That's a fabulous idea," Christie said. She grabbed a fork for herself, stabbed one of the little sushi pieces right through the middle, and put in her mouth. She looked up at me and smiled with her mouth full.

fufu rufu ('foo-foo 'roo-foo) adj., Spanish, informal:
1. anything that is gaudy, tacky, and loud. One can
find fufu-rufu clothes at the flea market and dollar
stores. 2. Cha cha or muy muy means the same
thing.

I KNEW SOMETHING WAS SERIOUSLY WRONG the moment I
opened the front door. At this time of day, my house was usually
bustling with activity, like a Macy's after-Christmas sale. My body
tensed up, expecting a *chancla* to appear out of nowhere. Usually,
dinner smells were in the air, music was playing from one of the
bedrooms, and the TV was blaring CNN, but now the house was
so quiet. After detention, I had gone shopping with Sheila to
help her find the perfect party dress. "I want something hot but

not too Christina Aguilera-ish," was what she'd said. I'd lost track of time, and now I was pretty late (as always).

"Hello!" I called out. Upon entering my parents' bedroom, I was blinded by a tangerine-orange color that was flashing before my eyes.

My mother was holding Marta's gaudy *quinceañera* gown up to her body. It was still the most repulsive thing I'd ever seen. I imagined someone suggesting to Sheila that she wear *that* to a party. I choked back a laugh.

"Es-tre-lli-ta," she sang. "Where have you been? We've been going over party arrangements for over an hour and a half. Did you have detention again?"

"Where's Dad?" I mumbled.

"He's in the back working on that stupid car of his." My mother waved me over. "Try it on for size." *Tía* Lucky was already taking out pins from her sewing bucket.

"Okay," I said, pretending to sound eager. I'd rather have dealt with the stupid dress than have gone anywhere near Dad when he was pissed off.

My mother shoved the gown into my hands. "Put it on. Put it on," she pressed.

"This thing is so . . . *fufu rufu!*" There were so many layers of fabric, I had trouble finding a way into it.

"Silly girl," my mom said as she helped me find the collar.

Tía Lucky was wearing a black leather skirt with a chain-link belt. It jingled as she came over and scooped the dress over my head.

I felt like I was drowning in orange sherbet. The gown was

so huge, you could have fit two of me in it and both of us would have had a lot of extra room. The dress kept falling off my shoulders. I hoped it would crawl away and bury itself in the backyard. Then I started flapping my arms: the extra-puffy sleeves looked like wings. There was no way in hell I was going to let Sheila or Christie get a good look at me in this fashion disaster. I'd have been so embarrassed, my heart would probably have stopped beating. "We tried to help Star," Sheila would say at my funeral. "I gave her some of my best clothes, but obviously she was already beyond hope."

My *tía* and mom stared at me with the utmost seriousness, like they were buying jewelry on the Home Shopping Network. *Tía* pulled and tugged on the dress. She had a bunch of pins sticking out of her mouth, and every so often she would jab a pin into a random part of the dress. Sometimes she missed. *Ouch!* And Mom just stood there nodding her head in approval, letting her only daughter get stabbed to death. "Estrella," my dad called out. "Is that you?"

My mother looked up at me from the *Nuestra Belleza* catalog. She was circling her favorite weddinglike dresses for teens with a thick, stinky red marker. But since I already had a dress, that could only mean one thing: she was going to try and force me to have other people be in my *quinceañera* too. The thought alone was too much, so I pushed it out of my head.

"In a minute!" she yelled out to my father without taking her eyes off the magazine.

Tía Lucky wiped beads of sweat from her forehead with the back of her hand. "All done."

My mom looked up and held my gaze for a second. "You better go."

I let the dress fall down to my feet and ran out the door.

The early-evening air felt surprisingly cool against my skin. Dad and Bobby were out back leaning over the engine of Dad's '68 Chevy Impala. If the living room was Mom's territory, the backyard was Dad's domain. It was littered with extra car parts and broken engines. It was also where my dad's prized possession—Chava, the classic Chevy—stood on bricks. All year round, my dad tinkered with her in the hope that she'd be ready for a car show. But for one reason or another, he was never able to save the money necessary to fix her up right. Behind my dad was the barbecue pit, which was always ready for an impromptu party or football celebration. And behind the Impala was a crumbling shed, where dad kept all his tools and stored all the exercise equipment he never used.

"Hi, Dad," I mumbled as I leaned on the other side of the car. Chava stood between us as if she were a referee in a boxing match. I glanced down at the engine and tried to avoid his gaze, but when I looked up, our eyes locked. This was not going to be pretty.

"*Mija*," he replied, sounding bitter.

"Yo, Shorty," Bobby said with a crooked smile. He sensed the tension in the air, made some excuse about finding a part in the shed, and disappeared.

"So, are you going to tell me what you were doing with that *cholo*?" My dad was so intimidating when he pulled himself up to his full height.

I stared down at his paint-stained work boots. "We were just going to school."

He snorted as if he thought I was lying. "School? Then what were you doing downtown?"

"I missed the bus, that's all."

"You know downtown is very dangerous. I don't want you around there, and especially not with no thugs."

"Dad, we weren't doing anything!"

"Don't lie to me!" he roared, nostrils flaring. "I know what I saw. How long have you been seeing this boy?"

"Dad, it was Agapito. You remember him. We used to take ballet *folklorico* classes at the Y." My voice cracked. A fly landed on my arm and I flicked it away.

His face softened. I hoped he was remembering the skinny little boy who had tripped and fallen over in the middle of the *Cinco de Mayo* parade. But then he shook his head and his face hardened again. "Estrella, you know the rules. No dating until you're sixteen."

"But Dad," I stammered. "Last time you said fifteen."

"Did I say that?"

"Rey had a girlfriend at fourteen," I pointed out.

"That's totally different." Dad smiled as if the answer was so obvious. "Bobby and Rey are guys."

"That's so not fair! Dad, I don't understand why you treat me like such a kid. I'm almost fifteen years old, and I can take care of myself."

Mom always said that Dad and I were exactly the same. We were always fighting to have the last word.

Dad lowered his voice and said firmly, "I won't have you throwing your scholarship away for some thug. I don't care who he used to be. Even nice boys grow bad in *el barrio*, and I can see he's hanging out with the wrong crowd now. You have too much to lose. If you keep your grades up, you have an amazing opportunity to go anywhere you want for college. You could go to Stanford or Berkeley or even Harvard if you really study hard. You know the rules of that scholarship better than me. One dip and you're out." He snapped his fingers. Then he softened up when he saw my frown. "Estrella, baby, we have dreams for you, and they don't involve ending up like your cousin Marta."

"So you want me to be a nun?"

"That's not a bad idea," Bobby joked, walking back with a monkey wrench. "You'd never have to worry about picking out an outfit."

Why was I always being compared to Marta? We were totally different people. I wasn't even thinking about starting a family. Secretly, all I wanted was to have a boyfriend, like Christie.

"But Dad," I said, ignoring Bobby's chuckles, "we weren't doing anything!"

Dad raised his hand. "No *cholos! Entiendes?*"

"Aren't you always telling me to think for myself? 'Be a leader not a follower.' How can I be a leader if you don't let me make my own decisions?" I asked.

Somewhere in the distance a dog was barking. Dad put his arm around my shoulder. "*Mija*, I just want the best for you. School should be your only priority right now. I don't want you to get distracted by boys. Promise me you won't see that boy again?"

I wanted to tell him that I didn't think Speedy was like that and that I wasn't going to follow his crazy rules. But as I looked up into my dad's soulful brown eyes, I knew that I couldn't say any of that. I was his baby girl. He'd worked so hard to help me get a better education. I couldn't let him down now. Someone was yelling out their window in Spanish, telling that dog to stop barking. It only barked louder.

"Okay, Dad," I said, putting my hand on my chest, like I was saying the pledge of allegiance. "I promise not to date thugs. Happy?"

He perked up instantly "That's my baby girl." Then he gave me his sly smile. "Hey, you're almost fifteen. You know what that means."

"I can get my permit and borrow the car?" I asked. I'd been dropping big hints around the house ever since they'd started offering driver's ed at SH. That way I could drive myself to school, go to ball games at Saint Ignatius, and go into the city with Sheila and Christie.

The back door opened.

"Your *quinceañera*!" my mother answered excitedly.

"Par-tay," Bobby said. He raised his arms in the air and did a corny little dance.

My dad patted me on the back as if I'd done something grand. *I've done absolutely nothing to deserve this humiliation,* I thought. All I was doing was getting older. For a split second, I wished that I could freeze time and remain fourteen forever.

"Well, come on," my mom said. "Dinner's ready."

"But what if I don't want a *quince*?" I mumbled under my breath as we walked inside.

Bobby was walking behind me and kicked the back of my heel. "You're crazy," he whispered. I turned around and he put his finger up to his lips. "Better not let Mom hear you say that."

Mom had set the kitchen table with mismatched silverware that she had collected throughout the years from various garage sales, discount stores, and restaurants. Our family life revolved around her kitchen. All the major discussions, gossip, and celebrations occurred here. There was something about the smell of warm food that made this the most comfortable spot in the house. My mother loved to cook. Today she'd prepared my favorite meal—rolled chicken tacos with rice and beans. The aroma ignited my appetite and helped me forget all about the horrible *quinceañera*.

"Where's Rey?" my mother asked as she brought a jug of Kool-Aid out from the fridge.

"He had to stay late at practice," Bobby answered. He rubbed his hands together in anticipation of the feast. "Yum, yum, yum. More for me."

I didn't realize how hungry I was until I put the first spoonful of beans into my mouth. They were so good. Oh, how my stomach had missed home cookin'. That sushi lunch had left me famished.

"So, *mija*," my mother said, "what do you think?"

"Huh?" I asked. My mouth was stuffed with chicken, corn tortilla, lettuce, tomato, and cheese. Hot sauce was dripping down my chin, too.

"Your *quince* dress. What do you think?"

I winced as if I'd been pinched. "Oh, that." I took a big gulp of Kool-Aid from my plastic *Finding Nemo* cup (free with any Happy Meal!), trying to think of something nice to say. My mother's eyes were shining, so I didn't want to offend her. "I don't know. It's kind of . . . old-fashioned," I said, looking down at my plate.

My mother's eyes just kept on twinkling. "You just wait and see when it's done. You won't even recognize it."

I was growing tired of her cheerfulness. "Mom, why can't I have my own dress?" If I had to go through with this torture, the least she could do was compromise a little. I thought about some of the cool dresses I'd seen earlier that afternoon at the mall with Sheila and Christie and fantasized about having my own designer dress.

My dad was studying me as if he couldn't believe his ears. *Maybe I'm pushing my luck,* I thought.

Then he spoke. "Listen, Reyna." I knew trouble was brewing. My father only called my mother by her first name when he was really, *really* serious. His face twisted in a knot. "I don't know if we can afford such an extravagant party right now."

That's right, Dad! I thought with a sudden burst of hope. *It's too much money! Cancel it right now!!*

"And why not?" Mom snapped. All of a sudden, her shoulders tensed up, and a vein by her right eye began to twitch. Mom was like a lioness, always ready to pounce on a predator who would attack one of her projects.

"I just think Estrella needs to focus on her studies right now," he mumbled.

"He's right," I interrupted. "I'm swamped as it is."

My mother absently brushed some crumbs off the table. "Nonsense. This is the most important day in our daughter's life— our *only* daughter. We have to do it right. The whole neighborhood will be there."

"Well, then, I want a new dress!" I demanded. I was beginning to resent my mother's coercion in my life.

"*Mija*," my mother gasped, as if all the air had been quickly drained out of her lungs. "What about *Tía* Lucky?"

I let out a hopeless sigh.

"She already offered us Marta's dress, and she plans to hem it all by herself. This is a great honor for her. You know how sad she's been ever since Marta deserted the family. I haven't seen your *tía* so alive and happy in a real long time. It would break her heart if you rejected her gift."

"But Mom," I pleaded.

"Enough!" Bobby cried. We all turned to him in surprise. "If it means so much to you and *Tía*, *I'll* wear the dress!" he said, winking at me.

★ *7* ★

> **dama** ('dah-mah) n., Spanish, formal: 1. It means unwed lady or girl. 2. It also refers to the female members of the quinceañera party, usually the birthday girl's best friends. It's a title of honor. The damas wear matching gowns, but theirs aren't usually as big and tacky as la quinceañera's.

IT WAS SATURDAY MORNING ON THE EAST SIDE, and the streets were buzzing with activity. Kids were racing around on their bikes. Teenage girls strolled down the block pushing cartloads of dirty laundry. Eager, T-shirtless guys watched them as they worked on their cars. The *panadero* had parked his van across the street and was busy preparing his racks of fresh-baked breads and *pan dulces*. *Doña* Vera was elbowing her way to the front of the small crowd that was gathered around the deliciously sweet-smelling van. The air was filled with the sounds of lawn mowers, *ranchera* music, and mothers yelling at their kids. "Juanito! Stop playing and get into the car! We're going to *la pulga* (the flea market)." Half an hour before, Mom had woken us all up and insisted it was time to go, but she wouldn't say where. So now we were all piled into Mom's minivan, driving through the neighborhood with no destination in sight.

"Now will you tell us?" I asked.

We stopped at a stoplight and my mother rolled down her window. "Margarita, good morning!" she called out to the large curvy woman in the full-size truck next to us.

"*Hola*, Reyna! Hey, kids! Beautiful morning, no?" We all waved to each other.

Yeah, beautiful morning to still be in bed, I thought to myself.

The light turned green and my mother kept driving. "Today is the first day of practice."

"Practice?"

"Yeah, kiddo," Rey added. "Thanks to you, we're all spending the next couple of Saturdays learning some stupid dance for your party. Way to go!"

"Ignore them. Your brothers are just excited," my mother said. "You remember how in Marta's *quince* they did a waltz. It's tradition. *La quinceañera* always does several dances with her *damas*. It's when you get to show off your talents."

"Yeah, but Mom," Bobby teased, "Estrella has *no* talent."

I gave him a dirty look. Then I stared at the back of my mom's head. *Damas?* What was my mother plotting? My palms were starting to sweat, and I wiped them on my faded jeans.

We drove down Story Road and stopped in front of the Mayfair housing complex. It was a gray two-story building with women in sweat suits hanging over the balconies like wet towels on a clothesline.

"Why are we stopping here?" I asked as my mother honked the horn.

"To pick up Teresa, silly," she said, not missing a beat. "You didn't think I'd forget to invite Isabel and Teresa to be your *damas*? Hey," she said to Bobby and Rey, "you guys get in the back with your sister."

"What? When did this happen?" I tugged on the seat belt that was across my chest. Suddenly I felt like it was choking me.

"Sorry, Estrellíta. It must have slipped my mind. There have been so many details to keep track of—"

"But Mom," I interrupted. My stomach felt queasy. Yesterday I'd thought I could get out of this. But suddenly it seemed so *real*. "I barely even talk to them anymore!" Why was my mother always doing things behind my back? It was bad enough that I'd had to go to Tere's *quince* and had bumped into Izzy. This was horrible!

"*Ah, mija*," my mother sighed. "I didn't think it was such a big deal."

"I *do* have my own friends, you know. I'm not some charity case."

"*Pues*, I don't know. You never bring anyone to the house. I thought maybe you girls could have fun, like you did when you were small."

Of all the people she could have invited, she had to ask the two girls who hated my guts! Yes, we'd been friends, but that was before I met Sheila and Christie. Before I started doing classy stuff like going out for expensive sushi lunches, lounging around in giant fancy houses, and going to pool parties that didn't have the phrase "community pool" on the invitation. There was a reason why they called them childhood friends.

Tere slammed the door of her mother's apartment. Her hair was high by drag queen standards, stiff and unrelenting on this windy day. She had charcoal-colored eyeliner smeared around her eyelids, dark purple lipstick caked on her mouth, and she wore a hot pink top with black stretch jeans. She looked like a *chola*, except for the fact that she had this big, cheesy grin on her almond-brown face. (FYI: *Cholas* don't smile.)

My mother let out a deep breath. "Well, it's too late now. Unless you want to tell her to go back home."

I gave my mother an irritated nod. I couldn't do that. Not now, at least—that would be too cold.

"Hey, guys," Tere said with a friendly wave and then hopped in the car. "Hi, Estrella."

"Hi, Tere," I mumbled, looking down at my Nikes. I suddenly felt hot and sick. I leaned my face against the dusty window.

Tere, Izzy, and I had grown up chasing each other down the aisles at the Lucky Seven Laundromat and learned our ABCs at Douglas Elementary. We'd picked out each other's first bras, practiced French kissing on our pillows, and even started our periods at the same time. We were like sisters back then. Izzy always had my back and was ready to throw down to defend me. I remembered how the other girls used to pick on me because I always knew the right answers in math class. They called me *fresa,* which was something you called a stuck-up brat or some-one who was preppy. But that had been years ago, before I got the scholarship to Sacred Heart. No one had called me *fresa* since then, except for Speedy the other day.

"Hey, Bobby," Rey said.

"Yeah?" Bobby replied.

"Are you hungry?"

"Yeah, I think I am," Bobby answered, giving him a sinister smile.

"How about a sandwich?" he yelled, and they both started squishing me until I thought I would burst.

Tere laughed softly, behind her hand. She was embarrassed about her crooked teeth and always covered her smile, which was a shame, because she had a beautiful face. My mother frowned and stopped the car in front of a little pink house with a white picket fence lined with red roses. She honked the horn as we pulled up front. The door opened abruptly and Mrs. Flores, Izzy's mother, poked her head out. "Just a minute," she hollered.

Then, from inside the house, I heard, "I'm not going! You can't make me!"

It had to be Izzy. I started fiddling with my seat belt.

Tere turned to look at me from the front seat. There was a questioning look in her blue eyes (she wore tinted contacts). It was like she was trying to figure out if I was the same ol' Estrella. *Not!* I thought to myself. She shook her head ever so slightly. I wondered if she was reconsidering her decision to be in my *quince.* Tere hadn't talked until she was in the second grade. At first, it had been only in the safety of our homes, during our numerous sleepovers, that Tere felt secure enough to talk. Then she became this big chatterbox at school. Everyone was shocked because it had happened so suddenly, but I wasn't. I knew better. However, now I ignored her stare and continued to look out the window. This was obviously my mother's party, and if she wanted Tere and Izzy to be in it, *she* could be their friend.

Next we heard Mrs. Flores saying, "Come on, this is for Estrella and her mother." Then it got real quiet.

Suddenly, Izzy appeared at the door with a big frown on her face. Izzy had streaked her long black hair violet. She wore a silver hoop ring between her nostrils, torn blue jeans, and a T-shirt that had the words *Chicana Anarchist* emblazoned across the front. Mrs. Flores stood in a ruffled apron, looking like my mother's twin, and cheerfully waved at us from the doorstep. "Have fun!"

My mother greeted Izzy by her full name as she climbed into the minivan. *"Hola,* Isabel."

"Hey, Izzy." Tere scooted over to make room for her.

Izzy glared around the van apprehensively. She mumbled something under her breath and silently stared out the window.

For a moment, the only sound was of Izzy biting her nails. Then Bobby burped real loud and shouted, "Yeah!" Rey high-fived him. Then everyone was silent again.

My mother turned on the radio. She found her favorite easy-listening station after adjusting the dial for a minute and started singing along with "Don't Stop Believin'!"

Three-quarters of the way into the third tune, the van stopped in front of my nana's senior center. OJOS DE DIOS was printed on the half-lit neon sign out front. It was her church's version of the Gray Panthers, a neighborhood watch group that patrolled the barrio much better than the cops ever did. The building also housed weekly bingo games and bake sales. It looked like an abandoned storefront with bars on the windows. Nana had started coming here last fall because of their free lunch program. I saw her standing on the curb, waving at us with both arms in the air. I couldn't help but smile at the sight of my crazy nana hopping around like a chicken in her orange-and-red flower-print housedress.

"He's here! He's arrived!" Nana cried out.

"What's she talking about?" Bobby asked.

"Oh, she must mean the choreographer." My mother smiled as she fixed her lipstick and puckered up in the rearview mirror.

"Mom!" I said in a shocked tone.

She continued to smile girlishly and fix her hair. "It's not what you think. He's a grand master *quinceañera* choreographer. He's done all the best parties in Mexico City. We are really blessed that he decided to do this one at low cost."

"Grand master. Wow, Estrella—you're *so* lucky," Rey teased.

I gave Rey an evil look as I followed him out of the car. Tere and Izzy stood awkwardly on the sidewalk. Tere tried to smile, and Izzy only glared off into space. Why was I being tortured like this? The fact that Tere was smiling made me feel even worse. Why was she acting so nice? The knot in my stomach tightened into a ball.

My mother pushed us all forward into the dark building. "Come on, girls. This will be an experience you'll never forget."

Nana's center was usually bursting with blue-haired old

ladies and rambunctious screams of "Bingo!" Today it was empty. The large windowless room had stacks of metal folding chairs on one side and smelled of mothballs. The pulpit had been unceremoniously discarded in the corner. A few pots of forever-blooming flowers lay carelessly on the floor, and light from plastic fixtures reflected off the pistachio-colored walls.

A tall, skinny man with long, thick, raven-black hair stood in the middle of the room, ignoring our entrance. He wore black leather pants, cowboy boots, a white T-shirt, dark shades, and had a white scarf wrapped around his forehead.

"He's been waiting," Nana said, taking my hand. "You're late." She glared quickly at my mother. "You will do everything that he says. Okay, *mijita?*"

Nana checked my face for understanding.

I was led into the center of the dimly lit room as if I were walking toward the guillotine. Everyone else followed quietly behind me. As I approached, I saw him better. My heart raced and began to pound in my head. The grand master was young. His five o'clock shadow (at nine o'clock in the morning) made his dark features seem mysteriously seductive. He smiled, then took off his sunglasses to reveal the most exquisite brown eyes and the thickest dark lashes I'd ever seen.

"This must be *la quinceañera.*" He took my hand like Prince Charming and twirled me around in a circle. "Gorgeous," he exclaimed. "My name is David Dieguez, but everyone calls me Grand Master D."

I couldn't help but laugh a little when he bowed before me. Who bowed? I imagined describing him to Christie and Sheila later. But then my face felt hot and I bit my lip when I remembered that I wouldn't be describing any of this to them later. They knew nothing about my *quince*. Guilt weighed heavy on my shoulders. They were my best friends. They were supposed to share this big day with me. But I was too embarrassed by the whole thing. Besides, I knew how they would react. They would laugh at my mother's plans and then laugh at me for going through with it. There was no way I could tell them. I was going to have to keep all this a secret.

Tere came closer for a better look.

"And you must be a *dama*," he said as he kissed her hand. Tere's chubby cheeks turned bright red. She curtsied as he continued down the row.

"This fine man here," he said, taking Bobby by the shoulder. "He's nice and strong. Perfect."

Then he turned to Rey. "And you must be the other brother. What a good-looking *familia*."

Grand Master D winked at my mother, who fluttered into a series of giggles.

"And"—Grand Master D stopped and turned around— "where is? . . . Oh, there she is." He went over to the doorway where Izzy was hiding. "The other beautiful *dama*."

Izzy looked stricken. Her deep-set eyes were about to explode. A small smile cracked on her face for just a moment.

Grand Master D addressed the entire group. "Now, people, I've been doing *quinceañeras* for a long time." He inhaled deeply, closing his eyes like he was about to meditate. "Each one has its own unique style and flavor. Now for you, Estrella my dear . . ." His eyes snapped open. "I see lots of lasers and smoke, drums and high-energy beats with a traditional flair. It'll be a clash of cultures, a true *mestizaje*. I'll call it a waltz*teca*. Yes, yes, that's it!" He chuckled, giddy at his cleverness. "Now, where is the *chambelan* hiding?" Grand Master D asked my mother.

Oh God, I thought to myself. I hated dancing in public. I felt so clumsy, and I never knew what to do with my arms. Even at the school dances, I preferred to sit and watch. That way I couldn't embarrass myself. I breathed in, hoping for some divine intervention to save me.

Grand Master D turned quickly and said, "The princess needs a prince to escort her on her magical night."

"Ah, yes," Nana said. "We're still working on that one."

My mother leaned over and asked, "Maybe we can ask your cousin Alex?"

"Mom!" I said through clenched teeth. "He's only ten years old!"

"We can get someone from my church. We got a new janitor," Nana suggested.

I shook my head at my mother. "I don't want a perfect stranger to be in my party." *And actually, I don't want a party at all.* I looked from Grand Master D to my mother and felt my quesadilla breakfast coming back up into my throat. *What the hell have I gotten myself into?* "Couldn't I just pick my own date?"

My mother's eyes flashed with a burst of anger. "*Mija.* You are too young to even think about a date! No boys! You can go without a date if you have to."

Suddenly, an image popped into my head—Speedy at our *folklorico* classes when we were kids. He was never graceful and always fell over, sometimes even when he was just standing still. I smiled.

"Partner?" Grand Master D asked. "Darling, you don't have to worry about having a partner. For the rehearsal, I will be your partner. But at your *quince*, everyone will be your partner!"

pena ('pee-nah) adj., Spanish, formal: 1. to have shame or be embarrassed by someone or something. For instance, when my mom wants me to make a total fool of myself by wearing Marta's horrible dress, I have pena. Or on one of those rare times when we all go out to a restaurant and after the meal Bobby leans back and lets out a giant, earth-shaking burp. Then we all have pena—except for Bobby.

ꝹID YOU SEE THE LOOK ON A.A.'S FACE when I got my geometry test back?" Sheila asked. A.A. was short for Anal Ana, the most annoying teacher's pet at Sacred Heart. She was always on our case. I swore she was a spy for the school.

"I totally thought her eyes were going to roll out of her head." Sheila laughed, leaning back on the huge pillows in Christie's game room.

Christie lived in a beautiful three-story house in the historic

Rose Garden district. Pink hollyhocks peeped out through the tidy white picket fence, giving the brick house a cozy country feeling. We'd come over to study after school, but all we were doing was gossiping by the fireplace. Christie's parents were at an HIV/AIDS fundraiser downtown and her older brother was off at Berkeley, so we had the whole place to ourselves. Her house was like a maze. There were five big bedrooms and five bathrooms, and it seemed like every room had a fireplace. There was even a studio out back where her mother made dried flowered wreaths for charity. It was so weird to me how their parents didn't feel like they needed to be involved in every second of their kids' lives. At my home in the barrio, I was never alone. Ever. There was barely any room to breathe.

"What would I do without you?" Sheila teased, referring to the math test.

I smiled big, my mouth full of ice cream.

"You're like my own private tutor," she kidded.

I laid back on the couch and put my feet up on the pillows. "Well, my services aren't free," I said in my best A.A. impersonation. "I accept MasterCard, Visa, and food stamps."

Sheila snorted loudly.

"Chris!" I yelled in a singsongy voice. "Where are yooooooooou?" She'd gone to the bathroom a while ago, and I was wondering if maybe she'd fallen into the toilet or something.

"Coming," she answered, walking lazily down the hall. Her hair was tied back haphazardly in a bun. She'd changed into a pair of boxers and a white tank top. Christie looked ill. Her face was pale.

"You okay?" I asked.

She made a nasty face. "I think it was something I ate."

"Or didn't eat," I corrected. Christie was on this wacky protein diet where she ate as much chicken as she wanted. But that was it, nothing else. She said she wanted to lose five pounds before the party. Crazy Christie. "This diet crap is absurd!" I protested.

"Oh, come on, Star," Christie said. "Get off my back."

"Well," Sheila said, "you can't expect us to just stand here while you starve yourself."

"I'm not starving myself, retards," Christie snapped as she plopped herself next to me. She looked at the bucket of ice cream in my lap and frowned. "I'm just trying to trim some off the edges. You saw the outfit I'm wearing to the party—it's hella tight. I must be getting my period or something. Look at my belly. It's disgusting."

"We wear the exact same size!" I said.

"Yeah, but you carry your extra weight in the back," Christie said. "Not in the front, like an old lady."

"You want to see a belly?" I pulled up my shirt and grabbed my pooch. "Now *this* is a belly."

"Wait!" Sheila said, in mock seriousness. "Check this out." She yanked up her shirt and pinched her love handles.

We both started comparing our fat and then we started laughing.

"You guys are idiots. You know that, right?" Christie smiled, grabbed her light yellow sweater off the back of the couch, and tossed it at me.

"Hey, no fair!" I took the sweater and threw it back at her.

"Sweater fight!" Sheila yelled. She ripped off her tight blue cardigan.

I love my girls, I thought as I used my pillow as a shield against Sheila's flying sweater. This was what being a teenager was all about. We had the whole afternoon to do whatever we wanted. Christie had TiVo'd an Orlando Bloom movie, and we were going to watch it and try out the new Kiehl's face products that Christie had picked up at the mall. After that, we were going to look on her computer for more party outfit ideas. Everything was perfect.

Then the doorbell rang.

Sheila glanced at the grandfather clock by the pool table. "Who could that be?"

We ran to the front door and peeked through the double-hung windows.

All I saw was the large backside of a woman with dark fluffy hair, standing in the templelike entrance. She turned, recognized my face, and brightened. My heart sank.

"Oh my God, Star," Sheila said. "I can't believe your mom actually got out of the car."

"Yeah, she's always in such a hurry," Christie noted. "Oh, how cute!" she squealed. "She's got pennies in her loafers. I used to do that in the first grade."

Why couldn't my mom just wait in the car like a normal person?

"Estrella!" my mother called out, waving at me excitedly from the doorstep. She was wearing those brown frumpy pants that did not compliment her waistline.

I moaned. "Sorry guys, party's over." I went back into the game room to get my stuff. Why did this always happen? Just when I was starting to have fun, my mother had to come and ruin it.

"Star? Is everything all right?"

I shrugged. "Yeah, I guess. I'm just not ready to go home."

Christie smiled back. "It's okay. We'll do this again. We still got to plan for the party!"

"Shhh," I said without thinking, hoping my mother couldn't hear through the door. Christie gave me a weird look. I rubbed my nose and looked away. "Yeah, we'll plan the party later," I said quietly, feeling glum.

When I opened the door, my mother had a huge smile on her face. "*Mija*, what took you so long? Hi, girls."

There was a fluttering in my chest, and I could feel my face turning bright red.

"Hi, Mrs. Alvarez, " Sheila and Christie sang like a chorus.

"'Bye, guys," I mumbled and headed straight for my mom's tacky minivan, which was parked at the curb. It pained me to see the van in this neighborhood, with its crusty bumper stickers and dirty windows with the words *Wash Me* printed across them in big letters. The car obviously didn't belong near the finely landscaped yards. I looked over my shoulder and saw that my mom was talking to Christie and Sheila.

"You know, maybe I've been to this house before," my mother said to Christie. "I think my friend Rosalba used to work here."

Christie's eyes brightened and my heart sank. "You mean Rosa! Yeah, she's our cleaning lady. She still comes here once a week. She's so great. My parents say she's the best cleaning lady we've ever had."

I marched back and grabbed my mother by the coat sleeve. "Let's go."

My mother waved. "Tell her Reyna said hi, will ya?"

Sheila and Christie giggled to each other and waved as they called out, "'Bye, Star!"

I wanted to die. I ducked my head and jumped into the van. *Tía* Lucky was in the passenger seat. At least she'd had the decency to stay in the car. Lucky had on an off-the-shoulder blue spandex top that I thought I'd seen J. Lo wear five videos ago.

"Hurry up," I grumbled. I just wanted to be away from here as fast as possible. It had been bad enough when some of the meaner girls at Sacred Heart had whispered, "There goes the maid's daughter" whenever I walked by. I didn't know what I'd do if Christie and Sheila started thinking that too.

"You're such a funny girl," my mother said. She grinned widely as she strapped on her seat belt.

Tía Lucky gave me a disapproving nod. "What's her problem?" she asked my mother in an annoyed tone. "She acts like she doesn't even want a *quince*. And who's 'Star'?"

"Oh, she does," my mom replied. "She just doesn't know it yet. Those were Estrella's school friends. Nice girls. They call her Star because Estrella is too hard for them to pronounce."

"The girl's name is *Estrella*," my *tía* stated firmly, as if I weren't in the car. "Those people should learn to say her name right or not at all."

My mother smiled. "Of course, Luck-y."

"That's totally different," my *tía* said, flustered. "That's my nickname."

"Well, Star is Estrella's nickname," my mother said, checking my response before continuing. "If she wants them to call her Star, then that's okay with me. As long as she knows that she'll always be my Estrellíta." My mother turned her head and gave me a big, toothy smile.

"Mom, you could have called."

"*Mija*, I couldn't find the number and we're in a hurry."

"But you knew we were studying for a big test," I said. How could she not understand? Didn't she know that telling my friends that she was friends with their *maid* might embarrass me? What was *wrong* with her?

"Next time can you at least call so I can meet you on the corner?" I asked.

My mother looked stunned. "But I thought you wanted me to get to know your friends. Isn't that what you told me the other day?"

"But not dressed like that," I muttered under my breath. I glanced up to see if she'd heard me. She had and was staring at me dumbstruck. Her shoulders tensed up as she focused intently on the road ahead of her. I felt sick to my stomach. What was wrong with me?

9

recuerdo (rey-'kwer-doe) n., Spanish, formal: 1. a
reminder 2. a gift given to guests at a baptism,
quinceañera, or wedding as a keepsake 3. It's usually
some plastic trinket with a name and the date etched
in gold ink on a ribbon. It's tacky.

MOM DROVE US TO THE GARMENT DISTRICT, which was
packed with old warehouses. We parked in front of a tiny back-
alley store that had a sign that read JUANA'S in hot pink lettering.
The shop was filled top to bottom with wholesale boxes of
quinceañera/baptism/wedding accessories. According to my
mom, Juana's sold the best party supplies at below cost. That
meant that everything was either damaged or too tacky for the
regular stores. Juana turned out to be a plump Vietnamese

woman with a permanent frown etched on her face. She had a short, boyish haircut and followed us around nervously. A cute lanky guy stood at the door, looking bored and smoking a cigarette. He looked like he might have been her son. I guessed he was there to make sure no one "forgot to pay."

"What you want?" Juana snapped in a thick Vietnamese accent.

I flinched at her tone and hid behind my mother like a five-year-old.

"We're looking for a guest book, tiara, and *recuerdos*," Mom said distractedly while searching for a list in her overstuffed purse.

"We don't want nothing fancy, but it has to be classy," my *tía* demanded in a haughty voice. *Classy?* I thought to myself. *Yeah, right!* I imagined what Sheila and Christie would do if they could hear my *tía* saying that in this place. They'd probably burst out laughing.

I grumbled as I followed the three women around the dusty, mold-infested shop. The place was so crowded, I bumped into a box. A ton of first-communion Bibles fell all over the aisle.

Juana gave me an annoyed look as she ranted to a small shop clerk. From the way the girl rolled her eyes, I guessed that she was probably Juana's daughter.

"I'm sorry," I said, trying to help pick them up.

Juana stopped me with an icy stare. I stood up and the girl snatched up the Bibles and put them back in their box.

Juana pulled down a box filled with tiaras. "Look at this." My *tía* picked one up and shook her head, throwing the tiara back into the box before I could even get a look. "Too plain."

"Mom, do you think I can wear a flower in my hair instead of a crown?"

The three women looked at me as if they had just noticed me standing there. Then they dismissed me just as quickly and dug into another box filled to the brim with heart-shaped sequined crowns.

I breathed deeply, trying to relax my weary nerves.

They made me try on every single tiara in the store. Some had tall points, some had swirls, some had dangling hearts—and they were all made of these incredibly sparkly stones that were not even remotely close to being real diamonds. My mom settled on the one that got the most ooohs and aahs from the other customers. An eagle-nosed woman with purple hair and a boisterous laugh pinched my cheek. She wouldn't stop gabbing about how pretty I looked in the crown. I couldn't have cared less and sighed when I saw the clock. Christie and Sheila would be halfway through the movie by now.

As the woman shuffled off, I looked at myself in the mirror and wondered what Speedy would think. First of all, he'd probably laugh his ass off and call me Princess or something. But then I imagined he'd look deeply into my eyes and reach his hand up and touch my face, gently. His hand would feel soft and warm. He would say how I really did look beautiful, and then he'd lean in and—

Whoa, whoa, whoa! Where was this daydream coming from? I couldn't be fantasizing about Speedy. He was a *cholo*, right? Except he didn't talk like a *cholo* and . . . he had deep, soulful eyes, and there was something about him that made everything else look a little different. I thought about what he'd been saying about factories and big businesses. It reminded me of how proud I felt whenever I went out to a fancy restaurant with Sheila and Christie. The only difference was when I was with him, I didn't feel awkward about not knowing something.

My mom smiled back at me. She'd seen me blush. Did she know? I wondered if dad had told her about the other day. Would she pretend to not know? Not likely. Despite the fact that my mother loved romance novels, she would never have approved of her daughter dating a *cholo*.

Tía picked out a white, puffy guest book that looked like a giant marshmallow. There was a picture of a brunette in a white dress with her hands folded in prayer on the cover. She had an "inspired" look on her face as she watched a dove fly in the sky. I wanted to gag.

"Excuse me," my mother called out excitedly. She waved the open book in front of Juana. "There is an ink spot on this! It's only fair that I will pay ten percent less for this, all right?"

"Fine!" Juana grumbled

My mother beamed. Getting a bargain made her day!

Then Juana started yelling in Vietnamese at the girl again. I felt so sorry for her, standing there, her dark eyes brimming with tears. I knew what it was like to have an overbearing mother always on your back. The teenage girl ran through a curtained doorway that led to the storage room, her ponytail flying behind her. She came back carrying three boxes. With all the scattered supplies, I didn't see her running back, and she bumped right into me, hurling trinket figurines all over the aisle. Again, Juana lit into her. I didn't understand what she was saying, but I knew it wasn't good, because the girl was blushing badly. Mom and Lucky gave Juana disapproving glances.

Instinctually, I bent down to help pick up the plastic figurines. They were covered in blue polyethylene wrap that crinkled when I touched it.

"Hi," I whispered. "My name's Estrella."

The girl seemed confused at first but then smiled. "Mine's Amy."

Juana snatched the box from our hands and presented it to my mother.

"This one very popular," Juana spat.

Mom held up a white, plastic pony with a flaming violet mane. It said HAPPY QUINCEAÑERA in gold cursive on its side.

Mom glanced at *Tía* Lucky skeptically.

"We got more," Juana declared. Then she yelled, "Amy!" over her shoulder.

Amy produced several other animal figurines, as well as miniature champagne flutes adorned with plastic flowers and colored ribbon.

"This one is my favorite," Amy said shyly, pulling out a thumb-size ceramic dove.

The bird of peace, I thought. "I love it."

The expression on Juana's face was so pinched, I thought I saw a vein pulsating on her forehead. "That is not for sale!" She snatched the dove out of Amy's hand and gave her a tongue-lashing before dismissing her to the back room.

"But that's the one we want," my mom said, putting her hands on my shoulders.

Juana was not going to budge. She crossed her arms and shook her head adamantly. "Not for sale," she repeated.

I was shocked by Juana's harsh disapproval.

"Mom," I whispered, "I want the doves." A part of me didn't really care which *recuerdos* I had. But the other part wanted to choose Amy's favorite—mostly because it seemed like we had something in common.

Mom gave me a frustrated look.

"Why can't we have the doves?" *Tía* Lucky asked, annoyed. She was tapping her fingers on the top of the glass counter.

Juana began to take deep breaths, like she was really trying to stop herself from kicking us out on our butts.

"My daughter is no good," Juana finally said. "She doesn't want to study. All she does is make things like this." She held out the ceramic dove.

"But it's really beautiful," I said.

Juana's face flushed with embarrassment. "Thank you, but they are not for sale."

I caught a wave of movement from behind the curtain. I wondered if Amy had been listening.

"Fine," my mother said with a frown. "We'll take these, then." She held up a plastic see-through bunny with furry ears. "Two hundred of them."

When we got to the car, I found Amy waiting there for me. She looked slightly embarrassed and gave me an awkward smile when she saw me. Then she held out her hand and put a ceramic dove into my palm. I tried to thank her, but she ran at the sound of Juana's voice.

★ *10* ★

la cucaracha (lah ʼkoo-kah-ʼrah-cha) n., Spanish:
1. a cockroach 2. It's also a famous Mexican children's song about a cockroach that can't walk. It's
got a funny little tune that's very popular. Everyone
recognizes it when they hear it.

I DON'T REALLY KNOW WHAT CAME OVER ME or where I got the
nerve, but that night I called Speedy. I got his number from Mrs.
Rivera's old class directory, which I found in a drawer in the
kitchen. Thank God Mom never threw anything away! (My mom
was in the room so I had to pretend I was calling Sheila—it felt
very undercover and romantic.) Before I lost my nerve, I said I
was sorry that my dad had left him in the dust the other day and
asked if he wanted to meet after school on Monday. He was so

cute about the whole thing having to be a secret and even came up with some code names—I was *La Chula* (The Cutie) and he was *El Guapo* (The Hottie). He told me that he'd meet me the next day after school and that he was going to show me a good time. And as long as we didn't get caught, I definitely was up for that.

But now it was four-ten and Speedy still hadn't arrived.

I was pacing around the corner of San Pedro Boulevard, where we'd agreed to meet, hoping he hadn't stood me up. I'd been so excited, I'd hardly slept, and all day today I'd thought I was going to burst. I'd been dying to tell Christie during science class, but after our last conversation, I'd decided to keep Speedy to myself.

I'd told my mom that I was going to Sheila's to study and that her mother was going to give me a ride home. If anyone I knew saw me right now, standing on the corner, waiting around, and hanging out with a strange guy, it would get back to my mother, and I'd be dead.

All of a sudden, I heard a car honking the *La Cucaracha* melody behind me.

I turned and saw Speedy behind the wheel of a cherry-red Ford pickup with monster headlights.

"What's this?" I asked, running up to the car.

Speedy leaned back, looking relaxed and confident as he rested one hand on the steering wheel. He was wearing a buttoned-up striped shirt and dark slacks. Instantly, I felt underdressed, and my heart started pounding. I hadn't expected him to get all fancy. Especially since I'd been up all night trying to figure out what to wear. I'd settled on a pair of black hip-hugging jeans and a peasant-girl blouse. I wanted to look, you know, casual. When Speedy saw me, he gave me a quick look up and down. Then he smiled and motioned for me to hop in.

He didn't have to tell me twice. I jumped in.

Speedy laughed as he turned onto Santa Clara Boulevard. It made me suspicious.

"So should I be worried about a cop pulling us over soon?"

"I didn't steal the car if that's what you're getting at," he said.

I rolled my eyes. "No, I was just wondering how you got your license already."

"I'm totally legal, Estrella. I turned sixteen a couple of months ago."

"But you and I were in the same class together."

Speedy kept his eyes on the road. "Well, I didn't know much English when my family moved here from Mexico, so I was put into first grade when I really should have been third."

"Wow, that sucks."

"Not really. If things had been different, I might never have met you," he grinned.

Speedy's compliments made me feel so giddy. I hoped he didn't notice it though.

"Where are we going?" I asked.

"Ahhh, that's a surprise. You like surprises, don't you?"

I thought about my mother's surprises all week and decided that I didn't like them after all. He must have noted the look on my face, because he gave me a warm smile.

"You hungry?"

"Sure," I said, wondering where he was planning to take me.

Speedy's car was crazy. A colorful serape covered the old leather seats that were falling apart at the seams. Tiny felt tassels hung from the window trim like stringed popcorn. They danced in time with the hula girl on the dashboard. And there was a pine scent coming from the Christmas tree deodorizer hanging from the rearview mirror.

"Nice car." I smiled.

"Like it? It's my uncle's. It was kind of dirty. That's why I was late." He smiled shyly. "Had to wash it."

"It's all right," I said.

"Your parents know you're with me?"

"Of course not," I joked. "You saw my dad. He'd kill me if he found out."

We laughed. It felt good to not have to lie around Speedy. He knew that my dad didn't like him, but we weren't bringing that up. The power of defying my dad made me feel like I could move mountains.

We chatted about music until Speedy parked his truck across the street from Fresh Choice.

"He gestured at the restaurant. "Cool?"

"It's cool." I was starting to feel a little nervous. *I am on my first date right now,* I thought to myself. I was so excited, it almost felt like a dream.

We were seated immediately. It was early and the dinner crowd hadn't arrived yet.

"C'mon," he said while taking my hand and leading me toward the freckled cashier with thick glasses. Suavely, Speedy lifted up two fingers. The cashier rang him up and handed us two red plastic trays. The bill came to forty dollars and some change. I was worried because I only had five bucks on me and wasn't quite sure about the "who pays" rule. Awkwardly, I reached into my back pocket, but Speedy stopped me.

"This is on me," he said. My heart gave a big thump.

I followed him to the salad bar. I wanted to kick myself for not knowing the protocol for first dates. Did I tell him I was on a diet? Or did I just eat small portions? I wished I could have asked Sheila and Christie. They'd have known what I was supposed to do.

I grabbed a small bowl and began preparing a salad. Speedy had disappeared from my side. Was he in the bathroom? I continued down the aisle and saw big heaps of mac and cheese, pizza, Chinese stir-fry, and a huge dessert cart where you could make your own ice cream sundaes or floats. But Speedy was nowhere in sight. I looked down at my salad, slice of sourdough, and juice, and exited the food aisle. A salad was safe, I figured. I didn't want Speedy to think I was a greedy hog.

Speedy was waiting for me in the middle of the restaurant. He was holding a heap of food on his tray. It looked like he had emptied the entire bowl of mashed potatoes onto his plate.

I couldn't help but laugh.

"*Qué pasa?*" he asked. He gave me concerned look when he saw my plate. "It's all you can eat. Go back there," he teased. "And don't come back until your tray is full."

"Okay, Dad," I joked and headed greedily back to the buffet. It was a relief to see that Speedy had a hearty appetite, because I really was hungry, and the mac and cheese was calling my name.

"Now that's more like it." Speedy nodded in approval. "I'm glad you're not one of those type of girls who's always dieting. I hate that."

I couldn't help but blush. I wondered if Sheila and Christie would have given me the right advice. They probably would have told me not to eat anything in front of him.

Speedy continued shoving green peas into his mouth as he talked. "My older sister is always dieting. She swears everything makes her fat. I hate to hear her talk like that, 'cuz I think she's beautiful just the way she is. What some people find attractive about a starved-looking stick girl, I'll never know."

If Sheila and Christie could've heard Speedy talk like this, I was sure their jaws would have dropped.

"Yeah. A lot of the girls at my school are like that," I said. "You should see them in the lunchroom with their Diet Coke and their sad little bags of baby carrots. But me? Well, I love to eat."

Speedy was glowing. "Me too. When I was a kid, I was always getting in trouble for sneaking food. You remember those Mexican round chocolates?"

"The ones used for making hot cocoa?"

"Yeah. Late at night I used to just bite into one and eat it like a candy bar. My mom flipped at first. She thought we had mice, but then she got wise when she noticed little teeth marks on it. She whipped me good."

"With the belt," I said, thinking about the thick leather belt Dad kept in his closet.

He shook his head. "Nah, she just spanked me with her

hand." He started to laugh. "Once I put wads of toilet paper in my pants to soften the blows. But my plan backfired. Imagine," he said, demonstrating the amount of paper stuffed into his pants, "a five-year-old boy with a butt the size of a mountain."

We laughed.

"Did you get the chili on the finger?" I asked. That was my dad's favorite child-rearing technique. My dad had put hot chili on my brothers' and my thumbs so that when we put them in our mouths, our mouths would feel like they were on fire.

Speedy's eyes brightened. "Did you suck your thumb, too?"

"Until I was like six." I laughed. "To this day I can't eat chili without thinking of my dad."

"Family," Speedy said, nodding his head.

"Family," I answered. "You ready for dessert?"

Speedy grinned. "I thought you'd never ask."

We jumped up and headed for the ice-cream cart.

"I swear not to drop any on your head this time!"

"Yeah! You better not!" I laughed. "Race you to the hot fudge sauce!"

Hanging out with Speedy was a blast. Before I knew it, it was time to go. Speedy dropped me off a few blocks from my house.

"That was fun," Speedy said, helping me out of the car.

"I had fun, too. You're nothing like I expected," I blurted out, then flushed at my candor.

"No?" He laughed. "What did you expect?"

"Oh, I don't know." Now, I felt hella stupid. I knew that I was blushing badly.

"You thought I'd act stupid, right? Like spend the whole time trying to look down your blouse or talking about what a tough guy I am?"

"Something like that."

We stood there at the curb for a minute, not saying a word. I wondered if he was going to kiss me.

"Well, I guess this is it," he said. "If you want to do it again, give me a call."

Speedy smiled real big, and for a second I thought he was going to lean in to kiss me. But instead he just reached out and shook my hand. He shook my hand! It took a moment for it to register. Wasn't he supposed to kiss me at the end of the date? Wasn't that a rule?

"Catch you later," Speedy said. Then he waved and got back into his *La Cucaracha*–singing car.

ALL RIGHT, PEOPLE," GRAND MASTER D yelled and clapped his hands together. "Enough chitchat. We have a *quince* to run here."

Bobby and Rey groaned. "I want to see two lines. Ladies on the left and gentlemen on the right. Move it. Move it!"

We scuffled around the chafed wooden floor and assembled into formation, eager to get this rehearsal over with ASAP. I stood uncomfortably still. Now I was the main attraction.

Everyone's eyes would be watching my every move. I was more than nervous—I was petrified.

Grand Master D pinched my chin. "Now, Estrella, I won't have you daydreaming on my watch. We're going to be busy, busy, busy. When is the party again?" "In four weeks," my mother sang from the sidelines, her cheeks turning bright red.

Yep, my mom was actually flirting with the choreographer.

"Ouch!" Grand Master D squealed like someone had kicked him. "That's not a lot of time. Not for what I want to do." He sighed and then sashayed to a boom box at the edge of the dance floor.

The music started with an explosion of drums beating wildly. Everyone stopped what they were doing to listen. It sounded like a theme song for some safari TV show. There was a crisp hornlike sound that made me think of elephants; then the noise abruptly changed into a symphonic waltz.

"This is hella cool," Izzy said, bobbing her head.

I flinched. *Izzy spoke to me and it wasn't a threat or between clenched teeth*, I thought. Maybe there was still a chance to make amends?

"It sure is different," I replied.

"Okay, ladies." Master D grabbed my hand. His touch was warm and soft, like a baby's. "Watch and follow. Bow to the east like this, then the west. . . ."

This guy is delusional if he thinks I'm going to do this stupid dance, I thought. I was so ready to walk out, but then I saw Izzy and Tere following the choreographed steps. Tere turned the wrong way. I smiled to myself. She still couldn't tell her right from her left. Seeing them both here, trying to learn the "waltzteca" made my heart expand. Only real friends would humiliate themselves like this for you, I realized. I wondered if they could forgive me.

"Nice," Grand Master D said, nodding approvingly. "Give thanks to the four directions before we begin. Now guys," he said, moving over to boys, "imagine that these are the last virgins of your tribe. Your job is to watch them, love them, and make sure that they are brought to the temple for worship."

"Worship? This sounds like horseshit to me," Rey snickered.

Then he leaned over and whispered something into Bobby's ear. Bobby busted up laughing.

Grand Master D walked up to them. "And what's so funny?"

"It's nothing." Rey smirked.

"Ah, come on, guys, we all love a good joke," Master D said coyly.

Now Rey was on the spot. Everyone was looking at him. There was no way he could back down.

"It's just," Rey said, looking to Bobby for help, "everyone knows that Tere is not a virgin."

"What!" Tere shouted.

"Gimme a break, Tere," Bobby joked. "You've got the worst reputation at Mission High."

Tere's eyes began to water. She fled to the bathroom, covering her face.

"Nice job," I spat at Rey and then chased after her.

I shoved open the bathroom door. The women's lavatory had been painted a dark bordello red. It clashed with the Betty Crocker yellow-checkered curtains hanging from the window.

Quiet sobs came from the stall. I knocked cautiously on it. Abruptly, the bathroom door flew open and Izzy walked in. She stared at me blankly; I stared back. Then the lock on the stall door unlatched.

"Come in," Tere said in between sobs.

Izzy and I squeezed into the tiny stall with her. Tere sat on the toilet, wiping her nose with her hand. Eyeliner had smudged under her eyes.

"You know, they're right. Everyone thinks I'm a big slut. But it's not true," she said. "Estrella, you believe me? It's not true. Stupid Rico, you remember him? My old boyfriend?"

I nodded. He was a boy with hazel eyes and a peanut-shaped head from our eighth-grade class. Izzy crossed her arms in front of her chest.

"I told you he was trouble."

"Yeah, well, he broke up with me when I wouldn't go all the way with him. Then he told all the boys at his school that we did it and that I was a big nympho in bed. He must have passed my number out, 'cuz all these jerks started calling. It got so crazy, I had to disconnect my phone. But it's not true! None of it's true!"

I reached out and put my hand on her shoulder. "I didn't know."

My heart felt like it had been wrung out to dry. Tere jerked back and shot me an indignant look.

"I tried to tell you. I must have called you like a hundred times, but you never called me back!"

"Oh." There was a pain in my stomach. It felt like someone had sucker-punched me. How could I have been so insensitive?

I thought back to all the times I'd made excuses and ditched Tere's calls.

"Izzy said that you were all stuck-up now. That you thought you were too good for us, but I didn't believe her. But then you never returned my calls. Why didn't you?"

All of a sudden, I needed air. Izzy and Tere were staring at me, waiting for a response.

"Well . . ." I was at a loss for words. If I told them the truth—that I really liked being a part of Christie and Sheila's rich, fancy world—then they'd think I was the shallowest person on earth. If I told them a lie, they'd see through it, especially Izzy, who could smell crap from a mile away. So I mumbled, "I'm sorry."

"You're *what?*" Izzy snapped. Her dark eyes were cold and unwavering. "We were best friends. Homegirls. Didn't that mean anything to you? You just dumped us, like we were nobodies, losers. And now you come back, ask for favors like nothing's happened. That's just not cool."

I looked into Tere and Izzy's pleading faces. They were hurt.

I put my hand on Tere's shoulder. "Guys, I'm really sorry about what happened. I swear I didn't know. All I remember about that time was that I was knee-high in schoolwork. Can't we just forgive and forget?"

"Don't tell me you were too busy to return our calls!" Izzy squared off in front of me like she was ready to charge.

Tere nodded in agreement and bit on her already short nails.

"But I was, I swear. You don't know what it's like to get into one of these private schools. It's nothing like public school, where the teachers don't care if you show up."

"That's crap and you know it!" Izzy cut in. "Fine, school is hard. So the hell what? It doesn't mean you ditch your friends."

"Come on, guys," I pleaded. "This is my *quinceañera*. Can't we just try to have fun?"

Tere sniffed. "No, we can't."

Crap!

"I told your mother I would do this party. I'm only doing it as a favor to her. Not to you," Tere said in a haughty voice as she pushed her way out of the stall.

Izzy gave me an evil smile and followed after her, saying, "And my mom is paying me twenty bucks a rehearsal."

Then Izzy poked her head back into the stall. "You've changed, Estrella. You're like this total stranger who happens to be wearing your body."

Izzy's word pricked like cactus needles all over my body. The school me wore makeup, styled hair, and had a cool disposition. The home me wore her favorite fleece sweats (with the hole just slightly below the crotch), a white tee, and her old dirty sneakers. The old me didn't have to try to impress her friends. Tere and Izzy had liked me just the way I was. I'd thought that when I started Sacred Heart the old me would disappear. In fact, I'd done everything I could to try and get rid of her. But maybe I'd done too good a job of it. Maybe she was gone forever.

I came out of the bathroom. Tere and Izzy were in the center of the room, whispering. Bobby and Rey were cracking jokes in the corner. Tere was watching them with wounded eyes. When Bobby started howling at one of Rey's jokes, her cheeks turned bright red.

"Jose Reynaldo Guadalupe Alvarez!" I said. Everyone looked up from the dance floor. "I will not allow you to insult my friends. This is supposed to be my big day and I won't have you ruin it with your immature games." And then I shut my mouth. Maybe the old me *was* in there somewhere, even if she was coming out sounding like my mother.

Rey and Bobby were staring at me and not blinking. My mother and Nana stood behind them, smirking. Grand Master D seemed bored as he scribbled in a notebook by the stage while Izzy and Tere shared confused glances.

"We were just joking around, Estrella," Bobby said.

"Well, your jokes hurt Tere's feelings and I don't want to hear them again," I retorted.

Rey turned to Tere. "Hey, I'm really sorry I said that. Okay? That wasn't fair and I didn't mean it."

Tere's mouth hung wide open. A fly was buzzing around the room.

"Jeez," Rey whispered under his breath.

"Now, if we're done," I said, turning to Grand Master D, "let's begin."

"Places!" he sang, looking relieved. "Forget the virgin thing."

"No, Grand Master D," I cut in. I looked at Tere and Izzy. "Keep it. We're all virgins." At that, Bobby and Rey turned bright red in embarrassment. Tere and Izzy stared laughing at them. And Nana joined in, her cackle rising above them all.

"Now where were we?" Grand Master D asked.

I replied, "We were just getting started."

★ *12* ★

escándalo (ehs-'kahn-da-low) n., Spanish, formal:
1. English translation: scandal 2. a situation or
event that causes public outrage 3. Actually it
doesn't even have to cause public outrage to be
considered an escándalo in my neighborhood. It
could be anything, like a tacky outfit you wear, the
fight your parents had on the lawn, Bobby getting
caught with a girl in his car. If it's good gossip, it
usually becomes un escándalo.

STAR," CHRISTIE SAID AS I CLOSED MY LOCKER after school,
"did you bring your swimsuit?"

My mind whirled. What was she talking about? Then I realized that I was supposed to go to a sleepover at her house. I'd totally forgotten.

Christie reshuffled her books and waited for my response. She was wearing a delicate necklace with a single diamond dangling off of it. Her hair was slicked back into a bun. "It's Friday. I figured we could go over plans and relax in the hot tub. Sound good?"

"Don't hate me," I said, closing my eyes as if expecting a slap, "but I forgot to ask. And I can't call and ask now or—"

"Oh my God, Star," Christie whined. "What's going on with you? Don't you want to help plan your own birthday?"

"I do," I said. "It's just . . . just . . ."

"Your family, right?" Christie rolled her eyes.

I didn't know what to say. Mom and *Tía* Lucky had picked me up all this week for *quince* preparations. There really was no need for me to be with them, because they made all the decisions. But if I told my mother that, she'd smack me. It was becoming harder and harder to keep this secret from Sheila and Christie, but I'd have been more than a little embarrassed if they'd found out I was spending my afternoons trying on tiaras with my mother while they were reading magazines and talking about guys.

Sheila met us by the front door. She also wore a bun today, but she'd added a zigzag part in her hair. Was there a hair memo that I'd missed?

"I'm sorry, guys," I said for what felt like the hundredth time. "There's just a lot going on at my house right now."

A silver Lexus SUV pulled up in the parking lot and honked. It was Christie's dad. He waved at us frantically as he talked on his cell phone. That guy was always in a hurry. Christie gave me a disappointed look.

"C'mon, Chris, don't be upset. Maybe I can make it over on Sunday or something. Okay?"

"Whatever." She walked quickly over to her car.

Was there anyone who wasn't mad at me these days?

Sheila and I stood in front of the school watching as other cars pulled away. I wished my mother would hurry up and pick me up already. Sheila checked out her manicure for ten minutes in silence.

"So, there's a lot going on at your house?" Sheila finally asked in a tense voice.

"Yeah," I said. I tried to think of something else to add. "Yeah."

"Sheila!" Her mother cried from the other side of the street. She was a slim brunette in an expensive-looking sand-colored suit and dark designer sunglasses. Sheila's mom insisted that we call her by her first name, Carol. It didn't feel right. My parents wouldn't have approved. They'd have said it was disrespectful. Carol got out of her car and walked toward us. She was beautiful. According to Sheila, she did yoga and went to the spa all the time to keep herself looking young. I wished my mother would take care of herself like that.

Sheila gave me a concerned look.

"I'll be fine." I laughed. "I'm sure my mom's just late because of traffic."

"We could give you a lift," Carol offered, checking her gold watch.

I shook my head. "No thanks. My mom will be here any minute." I looked down the street and prayed quietly, *Please, Mom, get here quick.*

Thirty minutes later, I was seated in the backseat of Sheila's mother's new BMW wagon. I wanted to shrivel up and disappear.

"You know, right here is fine," I said, pointing to a corner ten blocks from my house. My heart was beating real fast.

"Don't be silly, " Carol said. "It's really no problem. Plus, it's getting dark. I won't have you walking home alone."

"I can't believe I've never been to your house," Sheila said in disbelief as she studied my neighborhood. She looked over her shoulder and gave me a sympathetic smile.

It made me cringe inside. I couldn't help but hear a little voice telling me how pathetic my barrio was. It bothered me when I realized just then that being with Sheila and her mom made me feel inferior.

"Which one is it?" Sheila asked as she stared at an apartment complex adorned with graffiti.

"Don't people believe in streetlights around here?" her mother joked. I didn't laugh. Her mother cleared her throat. "It must be nice to live in such a colorful neighborhood." She nodded at the houses. "I've never been out to the East Side before. I bet they have good Mexican food."

I wondered if Sheila's mother felt as uncomfortable as I did.

"Um . . ." I pointed to my house. "This is it." Mom's van was parked in the driveway. *I could tear her hair out for embarrassing me like this*, I thought.

"See ya," Sheila said as I got out of the car.

Carol waited until I was in the house, honked, and then drove away.

When I walked in, Mom was seated at the kitchen table, talking on the phone and making an *escándalo*. "Estrella," she said, "*mija*, where've you been? You won't believe what happened to me today." Quickly she told her friend she'd call her back.

I slumped into the chair next to her.

"While I was going to your school, the van started making these really weird sounds. All of a sudden there was a ticking noise; then it started thumping and making a *geer-rump geer-rump* sound. I got real nervous because then the van started smoking. It was horrible. I had to get the car towed back to the house. I tried to get ahold of your dad, but he wasn't at work. By the time I got a cab to your school, you'd already left. Can you believe my luck?" She laughed.

"Mom, maybe it's time to get a new car," I said, annoyed.

"*Ay, mija*, don't be so dramatic. The car's fine."

"But mom, it's always breaking down."

"No, it's not."

"Well, maybe I should get a cell phone for emergencies?"

"*Estás loca.* Why do you need a cell phone?"

"*Qué es esto?*" My dad stormed into the living room, waving the tow truck bill in his hand. His work clothes were soiled with dirt and sweat stains. His rough dark hands had dirt underneath the nails and his eyes were bloodshot from lack of sleep.

"Oh, that's nothing," my mother dismissed. "I'll take care of it."

"Right. Just like you're going to take care of the fancy choreographer, hall rental, flowers, catering, and everything else you've planned without telling me!" my dad said sarcastically.

"*Ay, viejo*," my mother said in a soothing voice, "don't be upset." She walked up to him and put her arm around him affectionately. "This is a once-in-a-lifetime event. You should be proud that you can provide for your daughter. Don't you want to give her the very best?"

He crossed his arms in front of his chest. He looked like a boulder that wasn't about to budge. "Reyna, we're in way over our heads. I thought we were going to have *padrinos* help us pay for the event. We need to be sensible about this whole thing."

"Why am I going to ask a bunch of people to help pay?" My mother put her hands on her hips. "I don't want the neighborhood to think that we can't provide for our daughter. Are you saying that Estrella isn't worth it?"

"This isn't about my love for Estrella. This is about communication. We agreed to have a small party. Then I hear from Lucky that you're looking for a horse-drawn carriage. I don't know how we're going to pay for all this stuff."

"Mom, Dad, please don't fight," I said. I hated to see them act this way. It made me feel like it was my fault. If I hadn't been born a girl, they'd never have been arguing about this stupid party.

"This is none of your business," my mother snapped and ordered me to my room.

I put my head down and forced myself to walk quietly to my room. But as soon as I was safely behind my doors I started tossing my pillows around like crazy. None of my business! It pissed me off that she'd talked to me in that way, as if I were still in Pampers. I noticed that the argument had stopped. Tiptoeing to the door, I opened it a crack and listened. Nothing. I edged down the hall. Mom and Dad had gone to their room. The TV was on full blast. That meant they were still bickering. I grabbed the phone, pulled the long cord, and closed my door. My heart was pounding hard, but I forced myself to breathe deeply.

I kept all my important possessions on my dresser mirror: school pictures, concert ticket stubs, postcards from Christie and Sheila's vacations, and the page I'd torn out from Mrs. Rivera's directory with Speedy's digits. Quickly, I dialed his number. He was the only person I could talk to about my family. And I really needed a friend.

"Hello?" a little girl answered from the other end.

"Hi," I said nervously. "Is Speedy there?"

"Speedy?" the girl asked, confused. Then I heard a muffled sound, the phone dropped, a struggle.

"Hello?" Speedy said. Just hearing his voice made my heart thump extra-loud.

In the background, I heard the little girl ask in a real loud voice, "Who's that? Your girrrrlfriend! I'm going to tell mom you pushed me."

I laughed and suddenly felt more relaxed. I leaned back against my yellow animal-print bedspread. It was the same one I'd had since I was a little girl.

"Estrella?" Speedy asked.

"Yeah, it's me. Who's that?"

"Oh, that's my little sister. She's a pain in the B-U-T-T," he said.

In the background I could still hear his sister teasing, "Someone's got a girlfriend. Someone's got a girlfriend."

"Yo, be quiet!" Speedy yelled. I heard something drop, the girl yell, and a door slam.

I couldn't help but laugh at the situation. It reminded me so much of my own family. "Everything okay?"

"Yeah, I'm sorry about that," he said.

"Don't worry about it. I can totally relate."

"Family."

"Family."

"So how's everything going?"

"It's all right." I hesitated. Would Speedy want to hear all this? "My parents are driving me crazy. I can't wait until I turn eighteen and get away from here."

"You going to college?" he asked.

"Yeah, the farther the better. And you?"

"I don't know." He paused. "I don't know if school's my thing."

My heart sank. "What's your thing?"

"Well, there's the business, but that's just for now."

"I'm sure if you wanted, you could get a scholarship."

"You think?"

"Totally. Hey, what are you doing tomorrow? Wanna hang out?"

"Sounds good to me."

Speedy told me to meet him at the soccer field at La Raza Park the next day after *quinceañera* rehearsal. I practically flew all the way there. When I arrived, I found him on the field, playing with a group of guys from the neighborhood. The grass on the soccer field was yellowing and worn thin in some spots, but the guys didn't seem to care. They were running back and forth as fast as they could, letting out cheers and shouts. About half of them were shirtless. I got there in time to see Speedy (without his shirt) kick the winning goal. He was jumping up and down with all his teammates, and they proceeded to do a celebratory dance.

"Yeah!" I cheered.

Speedy's eyes brightened when he looked up and saw me. I blushed instantly. I had been trying not to stare, but Speedy shirtless was not a bad thing to look at.

He said something to his friends and looked in my direction. Then he pulled his shirt over his head and ran over to me, and I gave him a high five.

"Congratulations!" I said.

"Did you see that?" he asked excitedly. "It was amazing."

"Look at you," I teased, pointing to where his hair was plastered to his head. "You're all sweaty and stuff. I was planning to take you to a fancy restaurant."

His face dropped. "You were?"

"Kidding!" I joked. "Go on and get your stuff."

He ran back to his friends, pulled a pair of jeans on over his shorts, and ran back holding his duffel bag over his shoulder. "Where are we going?"

"Shh!" I said, putting my finger to my lips. "It's a secret."

He gave me a crooked grin and followed quietly. Behind us were the sounds of shouts and hollers, his friends starting another game of soccer. But Speedy didn't look back. We hopped on the downtown bus and got off at St. James Park, across from the courthouse.

"What are we doing here?" he asked, bewildered.

I gave him a wink. He followed. My heart was pounding as we climbed the concrete staircase and entered the lobby of the neoclassical building. Then we scrambled up the spiral staircase to the second floor. I'd never taken anyone here before. It was my special spot. I'd first come here on a field trip and had felt immediately connected with the building. Whenever I felt overwhelmed or frustrated, I came here to collect myself. The walls inside were painted off-white and there were a few pieces of antique furniture in the empty hallway.

"Are we allowed to be up here?" Speedy whispered.

"This is public property," I said. "Everyone has a right to be here." I leaned over the railing. Above was a domed skylight that revealed a blue sky with scattered white clouds. Down below there was marble flooring, a security guard, and random people going about their business. Speedy leaned on the banister next to me and put his face in his hands.

"So, what—?" he began.

"Shh!" I whispered. "Listen."

After a moment he said, "I don't hear anything."

"It's because you're not listening hard enough," I said. "Do you know how old this place is?"

"No."

"It was built in 1866 in an attempt to persuade the California government to re-locate the state capital to San Jose," I said automatically, blushing at how nerdy I must sound. I turned and looked at Speedy. He was biting his bottom lip and looked so confused that I had to let out a little laugh. "Sometimes I come here when I want to be alone. I like this place because it reminds me that I am part of something bigger." I smiled at Speedy. "I know it sounds totally dorky, but I want to work here."

"At the courthouse?"

I nodded. "Yeah. Look, touch this banister." I rested my hand on the rail in front of me. "How does it feel?"

"Like wood."

"Close your eyes. See with your heart."

Speedy closed his eyes. "Okay, now what?"

"Now tell me. How does it feel?"

"Like wood."

"Don't be such a clown," I said, swatting him playfully.

"Okay! Okay! Let me try again." He closed his eyes and touched the rail. "I feel . . . I feel heat!"

"Yes?"

"I see dead people," he said and then started cracking up.

"All right, Mr. Comedian." I turned my back to him.

"Come on, Estrella," he said. He grabbed my hand and started tugging on it. "I'm sorry. I didn't mean it. I was just joking. I guess I do that when I get nervous, that's all." He took a deep breath. "You know, my dad was always trying to show me stuff like this." He gestured to the building. "My dad loved to climb mountains. He was real quick for an old man." Speedy laughed. "Sometimes we'd race to the top and he'd always win. We'd sit up there all day, watching the clouds pass and the ant-size cars drive in zigzag formations. I felt like that giant with the beanstalk. My dad talked a lot like you. He always liked to say that we were part of something bigger." He stopped and then frowned ever so slightly. Then he shook his head. "That was a long time ago. I wish I would've listened more when he was around."

"Where's your dad now?"

Speedy smirked, but I could see pain in his eyes. "He died a couple years ago."

"I'm sorry." I winced. I didn't know what to say.

"It's all right," Speedy said. "I sure learned to appreciate my mom a lot more after that. I tell her I love her every day."

"You do?" I tried to remember the last time I'd told my parents that I loved them. I couldn't.

"Hell, yeah." He nodded. "Life is precious, as my uncle Raul always says."

"Is that the same guy who loaned you his car when we went to the restaurant?"

"The one and only," Speedy said, smiling proudly. "You should meet him. He's real smart, always dropping knowledge. He was a Brown Beret in the sixties, a real revolutionary fighter."

"Brown Beret?" I asked.

"Yeah, they were like the Black Panthers, but they were working in the barrios. They were real hard-core and had guns and everything."

"Sounds crazy."

"It was. Now he works as a youth organizer. He's the one who convinced Lobo and me to start our own business."

"I'd like to meet him," I said. "If he's important to you, he's important to me."

I closed my mouth quick, instantly embarrassed about sounding like such a sap. Speedy just smiled.

"I'm glad we're friends," he said, giving my hand a squeeze.

"Me too."

"You're not like any of the girls I know."

"Thanks." I laughed, a bit embarrassed.

"You're smart."

"No, I'm not," I stammered, turning bright red.

"And cute."

"Okay, enough with the compliments. You're gonna give me a complex."

He laughed.

"I like you, too."

His eyes brightened. "You do? Why?"

"Um, because you're funny, sweet, smart as hell and—"

"Cute?"

"Adorable!" I laughed.

His smile widened by a mile and he pulled me close. *Is he going to kiss me?* I wondered. *Oh my God!* I thought. *He is! He is!*

I closed my eyes and puckered up my lips and waited.

And waited . . .

I opened up one eye, then the other. Speedy was getting a head start down the stairs. "Last one down has wet *nalgas*!" he yelled.

No! I thought. He wasn't supposed to do that! He was supposed to kiss me now, like in the movies. But I had no time to pout. Speedy was already halfway down the stairs.

"No fair!" I said, trailing behind.

"No running!" the security guard called out after us.

Speedy was already at the bottom of the stairs and running out the door. When we were both out front, we decided to race to the bus stop. And then when we got off the bus back in the East Side, we decided to race to my favorite restaurant, El Grullense.

It felt good to run. This wasn't something I would have done with Sheila or Christie. It was goofy. But hanging out with Speedy made me want to do silly things.

El Grullense was an enormous place on the corner near the bus stop. With its sagging red awning, bright yellow tables, and walls covered in faded maps of Mexico and ads for Mexican beer, it looked just like any other taco place in the barrio, but it just happened to serve the best finger-lickin' tacos in all of San Jose. I figured it was a safe place to go because my mother was busy with Nana and *Tía* at the senior center, Dad was at work, and my brothers were at a football game.

We grabbed a table all the way in the back by the jukebox that played only top forty Mexican pop music. I sat facing the entrance. The place was loud as usual. I said hello to Gabi, a light-skinned cashier I'd gone to junior high with. "The usual?" she asked.

"*Sí, gracias.*" She gave me three chicken tacos and *agua de sandía*—watermelon juice. Speedy asked for two tacos made from cow tongue.

"I'm surprised that this is your favorite place," Speedy said, when we were at our table with the food.

I squirted lemon juice all over my tacos. "You are? Why?"

"I don't know. I thought you'd be too high-class for a joint like this."

The hot sauce seemed hotter than usual. I gulped down half my drink.

When I recovered, Speedy said, "I guess you're not what I expected either."

"Is that good or bad?"

"Good. It's very good."

My body relaxed.

We ate quietly for several minutes. Then I heard a ruckus outside the door, and my heart started pounding. Suddenly the place was overrun with about a dozen local teenagers dressed in blue and black, the local team's colors. They were waving their arms in the air chanting, "*Mi-shin! Mi-shin!*" Damn! The game had ended and the victors were coming to El Grullense to celebrate. Bobby and Rey would definitely be with them. Speedy was turning around to see what all the commotion was about.

"Speedy," I said very slowly, "I need you to do me a huge favor. If you ever want to see me again, you'll do it."

"Are those your—?" he began to say.

"Duck."

Without a second thought, Speedy dived under the table just as Rey and Bobby walked through the door. They threw their fists in the air, cheering.

The rowdy crowd cheered back at that "*Mi-shin!* Raaaah!"

Bobby and Rey started pounding on their chests like they were cavemen and whooped back.

"Yo, Shorty!" Bobby called out. He looked surprised to see me. "You heard!"

"Yeah," I said, getting up awkwardly. "Congratulations."

Bobby looked at the two orders of food on the table. "All that for you?"

"Yeah. I'm just here by myself," I said. I cringed, hearing myself, hoping he wouldn't pick up on the lie. "I was, um, very hungry. Have some?" I offered him Speedy's plate.

Bobby looked pleased and hungrily ate the taco in two bites.

"Hey, you," Rey said, shoving me over and grabbing one of my tacos.

I accidentally kicked Speedy and prayed that my brothers wouldn't notice. "Delicious!" Rey said, taking a bite. "I swear, El Grullense makes the best tacos."

"I think mom made some *carne asada*." I was hoping to tempt them to go home. Of course it was a lie, but I didn't care. I just had to get them out of here, and right away.

"*Carne asada!*" my brothers yelled greedily. Whenever my brothers had a game, their "macho man" instincts kicked in. All they cared about was eating, sleeping, and hunting for girls. It usually only lasted a day, but it was so annoying.

"Let's get out of here," Rey said. He didn't bother to rub the crumbs off his face.

"Right behind you, man," Bobby said as he finished my juice.

"Estrella, you coming?" Rey asked.

I wanted to say no. I wanted to tell them to get lost and finish my date with Speedy. But there was no way. Not while my brothers were standing there, waiting.

"Coming," I called out. But right before I hurried after them I felt Speedy reach out and grab my hand. He gave it a quick squeeze before I ran outside.

★ *13* ★

mal de ojo ('mal de 'o-ho) n., Spanish, informal:
1. a spell 2. a curse neighbors or strangers will use
to harm you 3. usually done out of jealousy or spite
4. You'll need to have a curandero (healer) remove
it with a limpia (healing ceremony).

IT WAS JUST AFTER NINE THE NEXT MORNING and there were
violins and guitars being tuned in my living room. And there I
was, standing in my bathrobe.

"What's this?" I asked.

Nana, *Tía* Lucky, and my mom sat mesmerized on the
couch, watching the ensemble of men with extra-large beer bel-
lies and fuzzy mustaches preparing to perform. The musicians
wore black suits with red ties and silver buttons, but none of

them fit right—it looked as if they'd rented their clothes just for today's tryouts. The jacket seemed a size too small on the guy with the trumpet and a size too large on the guitarist.

"Play one from my times," Nana demanded, clapping her hands in excitement.

The guys looked at each other, unsure of her age. Then they began to play "*Las Mañanitas,*" the Mexican version of "Happy Birthday."

"*Eso, eso, eso,*" my nana said approvingly. My *tía* was whispering into my mother's ear, while mom scribbled down notes anxiously.

"Come, *mija.*" Nana gestured. "Sit next to me."

I shook my head and sat on the arm of the couch.

"Want something to eat?" my mother asked.

"No," I said. "I'm not hungry."

She put her hand on my forehead. "That's strange. You didn't touch your dinner last night either. I hope you're not coming down with anything."

I hadn't been hungry since those tacos with Speedy yesterday. All I could do was think about Speedy, and my heart was swelled so big, I felt filled up. For a second I wished he could have been there to see all the musicians in their ridiculous suits standing in my living room. I bet he'd have gotten a big kick out of it.

My nana looked at me. She checked the color of my eyeballs and then patted my face. "You'll be okay."

Just as the group was about to go into their second tune, another mariachi band dressed in silver and white appeared at the front door.

My *tía* checked her watch. "We're running late," she mumbled.

"*Señora*," the freckled guitar player said, "it's cold outside. May we come in?"

"Of course, of course." My mother stepped aside so they could stand in the dining room. Seven musicians squeezed themselves and their instruments into the corner. Five minutes later, a *banda* group arrived. They had a tuba player, whose giant brass instrument filled up all the space that was left in the kitchen. When *El Peludo*, the one-man band, showed up, there was no space left in the house for his drum set, so he had to leave it out front. There were musicians practicing in my bedroom, in the kitchen drinking coffee, and even watching a soccer match in my parents' bedroom. We had mariachi players coming out of our ears!

The harmonica-playing lead guitarist/drummer of *El Peludo* was called Flaco, because of his long skinny body. Flaco was wearing a black bandanna headband, and he had two long braids that hung down past his shoulders and rested on his Ben Davis denim shirt. He started putting all of his instruments together, even though it wasn't his turn.

"One, two, three, four!" Flaco yelled. This had to be a joke! Then he started pounding on the drums with his foot like he was in a punk band and plucking chords like Dave Navarro. Between deep breaths and playing the harmonica, he started to sing a rocker version of "La Bamba."

Everyone in the house went stone silent.

I wondered if he was a recent escapee from a mental ward. But after a minute, my mom started bouncing up and down. *Tía*

Lucky was snapping her fingers in time to the drums, while Nana got up and started shaking her butt. She grabbed me by the arm. I started laughing, but she kept insisting. Soon we were all laughing and dancing together.

I don't know why, but I turned to look over my shoulder and noticed my dad standing in the doorway. Obviously, he hadn't known that our home was going to become the next mariachi festival. He stood there for a minute, speechless. I braced myself for the explosion. Dad had a reputation for having no tolerance for unwelcome guests. People joked that he should've been a bouncer. He was always breaking up fights and throwing out sloppy drunks at our family barbecues. But then my dad did the strangest thing. He turned around and walked out of the house. Without saying a word!

Afterward, Nana brought out a big bowl of *caldo de res* for everyone. She gave me a strange look when I told her I wasn't hungry, and then continued to serve all the musicians.

"*Mija*, go lie down," my mother commanded after the last mariachi band had gone. "You don't look good."

I sat down on the couch, leaned on the armrest, and tried not to listen to the conversation in the kitchen.

"You know what that girl needs," Nana advised. Mom reappeared with a wet cloth for my head.

"I said I'm fine, Mom!" I moaned.

She placed a cold compress on my forehead and pushed my head back on the couch. "What the girl needs is to rest now."

"I tell you," Nana warned, "it's *mal de ojo*. Well, how else do you explain it?" Nana quipped. "The girl was perfectly fine, then she stops eating and turns pale. If we don't do something quick, she'll disappear like a ghost. That is the work of the devil if ever I saw it."

"Nana, I'm sure it's just a bug or maybe it's the stress from the party. I know it's wearing *me* out," Mom said.

Nana shook her head. She wasn't ready to give up.

"Nana, who would want to curse Estrella?" Mom asked.

"It could be anyone," Nana spat. "There are lots of jealous people in this neighborhood. Maybe it's *Doña* Lisa, that shifty-eyed Filipina, trying to get back at me for winning last week's bingo pot. Or that sweet-looking *Doña* Coco. I know she's been trying to steal my mole recipe for years. Or it could be that old wino Jaime. He's always checking out my *nalgas!*" Nana rattled off more names and motives of possible suspects.

There was no talking to Nana when she got like this. Mom and I could not get a word in until she ran out of breath.

"Drink your tea before it gets cold," Mom ordered.

Nana sat down and obeyed quietly, shaking her head in agitation. She still wasn't done yet.

Just then, my *tía* came in from the bedroom carrying a brown handbag that jingled loudly. "Maybe she's in love?"

"Not my Estrella," my mother said dismissively. "She's too young."

I wondered if a loss of appetite was a symptom of love. Did that mean that I was falling in love with Speedy? I didn't know if I should be excited or mortified. My first love and I couldn't even tell anybody! This was horrible.

"*Qué es eso?*" Nana asked, forgetting all about the evil eye conversation.

"You'll never believe what I found at the Latin Jewelers," Lucky said. She pulled out a diamond necklace, a few thin gold bracelets, and a diamond ring.

"Va-va-voom!" Nana said. Her eyes bulged as she picked up the ring to examine it more closely.

"Is it real?" I asked, gawking at the diamondlike necklace. My *tía* had a habit of wearing cheap, gaudy jewelry and then trying to pass it off as the real thing.

"Of course it's real, *muñeca*," my *tía* said, trying on the diamond necklace. "I wouldn't be caught dead at your *quince* with anything fake." I thought about the tiara we'd picked out at Juana's but kept my mouth shut.

"This is great," my mother said, pulling me down into a chair. She was about to put the diamond necklace on me when she stopped and asked, "Lucky, how did you get all this?"

My *tía* was standing on her tippytoes, trying to get a better view of herself in the small rectangular mirror over the table. "Oh, Reyna, don't worry. I just put it on my credit."

The front screen door slammed. My dad stood there looming over us. His bulky size blocked the sun behind him like a storm cloud.

"*Ay, viejo*," my mom scolded affectionately, "don't let the door slam. It scares me to death."

My dad said nothing. He watched the women of his extended family play dress-up like little girls. I sat glued to my chair, sensing the tension that had come in with him.

"*Qué es esto?*" he asked, pointing at the jewelry on the table.

My mother came up to him and patted his shoulder

affectionately. "Lucky saved the day. I totally forgot about Estrella's jewelry and she—"

"*No quiero esto en mi casa!*" he yelled, shoving the pieces of jewelry haphazardly into the handbag. "Here," he said to a stunned Lucky. "We don't want your help."

"Manuel!" my mother cried. "What are you doing? Have you been drinking?"

Lucky took the bag and made an excuse about taking Nana home as they scrambled for their things. They both knew my dad's temper and didn't want to be on the receiving end of it. Nana and *Tía* wouldn't be back until the storm had passed. My dad was usually a funny, easygoing guy, but I could tell he'd reached his limit.

When my *tía* left, my mom struck back. "Damn it, Manuel! What the hell is wrong with you?"

"What's wrong with *me*? Are you crazy? I'm just trying to save our family from going bankrupt. If I left this all up to you, we'd be out on the street by now!"

"How could you say such a thing! You're making me sick!"

As I sat and watched them argue, I felt very numb. When I was a kid, I used to hide and cry myself to sleep whenever my parents fought. But over the years, I'd gotten used to it. All the fights were about the same thing—money, or the lack of it. My mom had been really poor as a little girl and believed that money was for enjoying in the here and now. Dad was all about saving money for a rainy day. He'd tried to teach my mother how to balance the checkbook. My mother had never understood it and continued to overdraw the accounts. She was always surprised when the electricity was cut off.

"What do you call that little musical recital going on here this morning? I thought we decided to get a *trio*, not a whole mariachi band!"

"Oh well," My mother smiled meekly. She was caught. I couldn't help but feel happy. Maybe now mom would realize how ridiculous this *quinceañera* was getting and just reduce it to a small party.

"Lucky and I had this idea," my mom said innocently.

"Oh, so now you decide everything with your sister, the woman who's still twenty thousand dollars in debt for her own daughter's *quinceañera*. What were you thinking, inviting all those bands over? I know they don't do house calls for free."

My mother shook her head. "Manuel, you don't understand. Once again, you've totally blown the situation out of proportion. And it isn't twenty thousand, it's eighteen."

"Twenty, eighteen—what's the difference?" he grumbled.

Obviously, she was plowing forward with her plans without stopping to think about what she was doing. Couldn't she see that this party was getting out of control?

"Mom!" I said urgently. I just wanted her attention for a second to tell her how I felt.

But my mom totally ignored me. "Manuel, I won't talk to you when you're acting unreasonable. I have things to do and I can't waste my time with your nonsense." She grabbed her purse. "Come on, Estrella. We have an appointment that we can't miss."

She grabbed my arm and dragged me outside. I heard my father shouting as we left, "Do I really have to hire seven musicians just to prove how special my daughter is? Their suits don't even fit right!"

hijole (ee-'ho-lay) Spanish expression, very informal:
1. It's kind of like saying, "Oh my God!" when you're
really excited or surprised, or even mad. Its intended
meaning is taken from its context. Sometimes when
Rey sees a pretty girl, he will elbow Bobby and say,
"Hijole, Bobby! Look at her! I'm going to go talk to
her!" This is what he says right before the girl ignores
him and keeps walking.

HIJOLE, ESTRELLA, STOP SQUIRMING," my mother said.

That was easy for her to say. She wasn't the one striking an
Egyptian pose. "But mom," I said, "my arms feel like bricks."

"Shhh!" my *tía* interrupted. Then she turned and apolo-
gized profusely to Leif, the blond Rastafarian artist who was
sketching my figure. "I've always loved your work, ever since
the Avon convention at the Hyatt. Your sculpture was simply
breathtaking." Her eyes were glazing over. "I stared at it for

hours. It was *so* beautiful. I just had to have one for my favorite niece's birthday."

By the way, I was her *only* niece.

"I knew that this would be the icing on the cake for her party. Everyone will be raving about it for years." Lucky clapped her hands in excitement. "Thank you so much for doing this on such short notice."

Leif just nodded as he continued sketching me. He was leaning back in a green beanbag chair and wore an orange pantsuit with Birkenstocks. We were in his cluttered houseboat living room/kitchen. His work studio, which was also a cold-storage room (obviously) was on an upper deck.

I could not believe that my mother had agreed to a personalized life-size ice sculpture of me! This was ridiculous. I would be the laughingstock of the entire school if anyone found out. I'd seen what those things looked like when they melted. My face would be all distorted and smeared. My nose would be on my chin and my boobs at my knees!

Leif grabbed my hand. "I'd like to try out a couple of more poses before I get started."

I was standing there posing like a model in my favorite fleece sweats and a blue T-shirt, with my hair in a messy ponytail. If it hadn't been so embarrassing, it would have been funny. I gave my mom a pleading look that could have been interpreted as *Please, no more.*

"I think she should be kneeling in prayer," my *tía* suggested.

"How about we do her with her arms open for an embrace?" my mother asked.

"How about I do a karate chop?" I mumbled. No one noticed except for Leif, who looked at me and winked. I smiled back.

The sun was setting when we headed home. It was past dinnertime, and we were all hungry and exhausted. As we drove through the Rose Garden district, I wondered if Sheila was over at Christie's house. I felt horrible about ditching them on Friday.

"Mom, do you think you could drop me off at Christie's?" I asked.

"Okay, *mija*," she said after a minute. "Just promise me you'll be back in a few hours. We have an appointment at nine to talk with the priest."

"I promise."

She dropped me off in front of Christie's house and waited as I walked up the path and rang her bell. Christie poked her head out the window and gasped.

"You're here!" she said as she threw open the door and pulled me inside before I could even wave good-bye to my mom.

"Girl, you are so lucky you came," Christie said. "We were all ready to cancel the party." She led me out back to a large backyard filled with fruit trees and the scent of lavender. The brick patio was lit with tiki torches. Sheila was lounging in a reclining chair, smoking a cigarette. I noticed that they both had their hair done in loose, sexy waves, like they'd gone to the salon earlier today. The hairstyle made Christie's blond locks look sultry. Sheila looked ready for a party. I couldn't help but feel a prick of jealousy.

I plopped myself into the chair next to Sheila.

"So where've you been?" Christie said haughtily.

"C'mon guys," I said. "I know I've been a total flake."

"You have," Sheila snapped. "What's up, Star? I thought you liked parties and having fun. Now all you do is sit at home with your *parents*." She said the word *parents* like someone else might say the words *dog poop*.

"I *do* like parties," I said.

"Well then," Christie replied, "what's up?"

"It's just that . . ." I sat for a minute, looking straight at them. They looked so prim, with their picture-perfect profiles and beautiful houses. *But they're also your friends*, I told myself. "Remember when I told you guys about that stupid party I had to go to with my folks?"

They both nodded seriously.

"Well, you see, it was actually kind of like this big deal. They rented a limo and the reception was at the Hyatt downtown."

"Oookay," Christie said.

They were looking at me, confused, like they were thinking, *Why are you telling us this?*

I continued. "This party was for this girl I knew a long time ago. Her parents got a band, a huge cake, and everyone wore puffy gowns."

"Like a debutante ball?" Sheila asked.

"Yeah. Well, sort of," I spoke quickly. "It's like this Mexican thing. It's all traditional and whatever." I took a deep breath and let it out. My heart was pounding so hard, it felt like it was going to jump out of my chest. I breathed in and then opened my mouth and all in one rush I said,

"Anywaymyparentsarethrowingoneforme."

"Huh?" Sheila looked at me and blinked.

"My parents," I said. "They're having one of those parties for me."

We were all silent for a second.

"It's supposed to be when a girl's turning fifteen and she's becoming a woman or something," I blushed as I heard myself say "becoming a woman."

Sheila and Christie turned and looked at each other and then burst out laughing.

"Star, you're *becoming a woman?*" Christie asked with a grin. "We had no idea! Why didn't you tell us?"

"*Oh, look, our little Star is blossoming,*" Sheila cooed in a fake high voice. "*We are so proud of you, you woman, you.*"

I felt my face turning bright red. "Come on, guys," I said, trying to force a laugh. "It's not like *that*; it's like . . . It's not really that lame. It's actually kind of cool." I stopped. What was I saying? "It's tradition."

Sheila and Christie both looked at me like I was speaking Spanish.

"Wait, so you're having this big traditional woman party?" Sheila asked.

"Yes," I said.

"Why didn't you tell us before?" Christie asked.

"Well, you see, it's kind of my mother's thing. I didn't tell you guys about it because I never wanted one in the first place. I was trying to convince her not to do it because it's sort of dumb. But you know how mothers can be when they get something in their heads."

"So why don't you want it?" Sheila asked, taking a long drag off her cigarette.

"Well, my mom's out of control. She's making me wear this god-awful dress with a crown. It's really tacky." I rolled my eyes.

"A *crown?*" Sheila let out a laugh. "She wants you to wear a *crown* to your birthday party? You must be joking."

I shook my head.

"Is there going to be a DJ?" Christie asked.

"I don't know. I think my mom's getting mariachis."

Christie crossed her eyes in distaste. "Mariachis are cool for *Cinco de Mayo* but not for your birthday."

"Yeah, Star," Sheila said. "This is *your* birthday."

I nodded, feeling relieved that I'd finally told my friends the truth. But I also felt strangely annoyed. Sure, *I* was allowed to think my *quince* was dumb, but for some reason, it really bothered me that they were agreeing.

"Well, I don't know what to do," I said, feeling frustrated. "My mom puts so much pressure on me. I have to be the perfect daughter and do everything that she wants. She never asks for my input. Then there's my aunt and grandmother, who are always at the house scheming. You'd swear it was *their* party, with all the fuss they're making."

Christie came over to me and put both of her hands on my shoulders. "Star, this is your life, remember that. Your mother only gave birth to you. She doesn't own you. Parents will run your life if you let them. I remember when my mom wanted me to be a pop star." Christie rolled her eyes. "I'm totally serious. She spent, like, thousands of dollars to send me to these fancy singing programs at"—she paused and then spoke in a fake upper-class accent—"*the Aaron Welles Music Academy,* even though I couldn't hold a tune. My mother thought I'd become the next American Idol. It was so embarrassing. Whenever company was over, she'd make me sing all these songs for them. It all ended when a cute boy came over for dinner with his family and she tried to force me to sing a mother-daughter duet. That was the first time I stood up to her. She's never asked me to sing for company again."

"And aren't we'll thankful for that," Sheila cracked.

"Ha ha," Christie replied. "But seriously, Star, you've got to stand up for yourself. Only you know what it is that makes you happy. So don't let anyone else tell you otherwise."

"Right on," Sheila agreed, raising her can of Diet Coke in the air.

I thought about how happy I was when I was with Speedy. Maybe Speedy could even be my partner at my *quinceañera?* That would actually make the *quince* kinda fun.

"Maybe you could save this party after all," Sheila suggested. "Get your folks to make it a little less traditional and ask them to get you a stretch Suburban. Those cars are so hot. And then we can even ride to the city afterward. Wouldn't that be beyond?"

"I don't know," I said flatly.

"Well," Christie said, "we *were* going to wait. But seeing as our party is next weekend, I guess it couldn't hurt if we gave you your birthday gifts early."

"What?" I asked. My head felt like it was spinning. "You heard her," Sheila hooted. "Christmas is coming early this year!"

"Huh?" I couldn't believe that they were still going to go through with the party.

"C'mon, dorko," Sheila said as we made our way upstairs to Christie's bedroom. As weird as I felt, a little twinge of excitement started to build in my stomach.

Downstairs the rooms were decorated with English country-style charm and filled with antique furniture that made the house feel more like an inn or a B&B. But Christie's room was definitely all her. She'd painted the walls with her favorite tones: red and orange, which represented passion and spice.

Christie's bed was covered with DKNY, Armani, and Tommy Hilfiger shopping bags. *I guess I missed the sale*, I thought as Christie handed me a gift.

I couldn't believe I was holding a beautifully wrapped Versace box. "What's this?"

Christie smiled. "I know you didn't have time to buy yourself a new outfit for the party."

She was lying of course: she knew I didn't have the money to buy an expensive outfit.

I opened it up and pulled out an amazing turquoise rose-print dress. "It's beautiful!"

"It's the same dress Jessica Simpson wore on the cover of *US* magazine three weeks ago," Sheila squealed as she felt the material.

"I think it'll look better on you," Christie said. "You have the color for it."

"Jessica had a bad tan." Sheila snickered.

"I love it," I said. "I *really* love it."

"And this is from me and my mom." Sheila placed a small box wrapped in pink tissue in my hands.

Inside the box was a silver Sony Ericsson camera phone. It was so cute, and it fit in the palm of my hand. I'd always wanted my very own cell. "It's prepaid," Sheila added. Then she showed me how to use the camera and took my picture. "It was my mom's idea—you know, in case of emergencies."

"I can't accept this," I said. Actually, I felt ashamed for even wanting it.

Sheila rolled her eyes. "God, Star. We both have cell phones already, so I thought you'd want to have one, too. It's not a huge deal. It's just a gift."

"I'm sorry. You're right." I gave her a hug. "Thank you."

I already knew just who I was going to call first.

★ *15* ★

> **vago** ('vah-go) n., Spanish, slang: 1. a vagabond 2. a guy who does nothing but hang out on the street. My mom calls all the boys on the street vagos, and she calls me a vaga when I hang out too much with Sheila and Christie.

JUST HOLDING THE SILVER PHONE IN MY HAND made me feel different. Like I was instantly richer and fancier. I couldn't believe that it was actually mine. "Hello?" Speedy's voice always sounded so good.

"Guess what I'm doing?"

"I don't know," he replied. "Can you give me a hint?"

"Well, I'm obviously talking to you."

"Right. I got that part!"

"And I'm in motion!"

"Um. You exercising to the TV?"

"No . . ."

"Running around the kitchen? Jumping on your bed?"

"No, Einstein. I'm on my new cell phone!"

"Cell phone? Wow, that's hot. Where you at?"

"I'm at La Raza Park. Want to meet up?"

"Sure."

"I'll be waiting."

I sat down at one of the rickety picnic benches. It was covered in graffiti—*Tony loves Gina, Casper was here,* and someone had drawn a bunch of *XIVs*.

As I sat and waited, I thought about calling my mom. There was no way I could tell her who I was actually with or what I was actually doing. If she knew I was with Speedy, she'd probably throw the *chancla* so hard it would reach me through the phone! I could tell her that the bus had broken down or something. But I felt really bad about lying. Maybe I could tell her that I needed more time for myself. Like Christie had said, I had to make myself happy.

Suddenly, Speedy raced by on his bike. What was it about this guy? He was so handsome, it made my teeth hurt. His dark jeans, crisp white shirt, and backwards cap were sloppy, but in a cute way. His bronzed skin was glowing. Speedy smiled as he did a wheelie in front of me. He pulled up to my picnic bench and stopped.

"Hey there, hotshot," I teased. Then I flinched because I sounded so corny.

He leaned his bike against the bench and sat down beside me. "Cool trick, huh?"

I nodded, feeling shy at first. But Speedy was grinning so big, I felt all my nervousness fade.

"So show it to me," he said impatiently, like a little boy on Christmas Day.

"Okay, okay," I said as I reached into my bag. "Ready? Here it is."

"Wow! That's very nice," he said, snatching it out of my hand.

"You can even take pictures."

"Really? Let's see." He pointed the camera at me. *Snap.* He pointed it at himself, smiled with a goofy grin, and snapped another. Then he said, "C'mere," and gestured for me to sit closer to him. I leaned back and he put his arm around me. My heart was racing so fast. His cologne smelled like a cool breeze and it made my head swoon.

"Smile!"

Click. He took another picture. I hadn't been looking at the camera!

"Hey, I wasn't ready. Let me see that." I took the camera from him and checked out the picture. He was smiling brightly, looking adorable (as always), and I was gazing at him all googly-eyed like I was in love with him or something.

"Hey, let me see that," he said, reaching for the cell.

"No!" I held the phone close to my chest.

"Oh, come on. Don't be shy," he said slyly.

"No!" I said again. I had to erase the picture. *Speedy can't see this*, I thought as I got up and dashed across the field.

"You don't want me to come after you!" he warned.

I kept running toward the playground ahead. Maybe I could figure out how to delete the photo before he got here. I would be so embarrassed if he saw the picture. I started pressing menu buttons frantically. There had to be a delete button on here somewhere! But before I could figure it out, Speedy grabbed me from behind. Actually, he stumbled into me and we both tumbled down into the soft grass. We tried to get up and bumped heads. Then we fell back down, cracking up with laughter.

Speedy crawled over to me. "You all right?"

"Yeah." I giggled. "I'm fine." I was lying on my back, looking up at the darkening sky. Then Speedy leaned over me and my breath caught in my throat. He had a piece of grass stuck in his hair. I raised my hand to pick it out. He stopped me and held onto my hand, and my ears started pounding.

"What?" I asked nervously.

"Shhh," he said softly, bringing his finger to his lips.

Oh my God! I wanted to scream. He was so close that I started worrying about the huge zit on the side of my forehead. Could he see it? Why was he still staring at me? *Maybe he's delirious?* I thought.

"Did you hit your head when you fell?" I asked suddenly.

Speedy gave me a really confused look. I couldn't stand the tension anymore and closed my eyes.

"What are you thinking?" He combed loose locks of my hair back behind my ear.

"Thinking? I'm not thinking about anything."

"Oh, come on. I can hear your brain ticking," he said. Then he made clicking sounds and bobbed his head as if it were a clock.

"I guess," I said, shoving him back a little, "I was thinking about stuff."

"Ooh, stuff. Sounds juicy."

"You haven't changed a bit." I laughed as I swatted him on the arm.

"That's more like it," he grinned. "You need to smile more often. I remember you were always so serious as a little girl. You always had your head in the books."

"Yeah, well some of us have to work hard at getting out of the barrio."

Speedy did a double take, as if he weren't sure he'd heard me correctly. "Why do you want to leave the barrio?" he asked.

"Hello? Do you know where we live?" I said, pointing to the crumbling concrete, graffitied signs, and abandoned shopping carts around us. "This is not the best neighborhood."

"But it's *our* neighborhood." He sounded hurt, as if I'd offended a family member.

"Come on, Speedy," I said. "Don't get all sensitive on me now. We both know that this place is wack. It's so small, everyone is always in your business, and no one ever takes the time to take those carts back to the store. It's like all the people here have given up on life and are just trying to get by."

"That's so unfair," he said.

"Yeah, well you should see my friend's house in Willow Glen. Her block is so beautiful. Everyone takes care of their houses and the street is always clean." Speedy turned away from me and began pulling grass out by its roots. "Is everything okay?"

"I could ask the same thing of you. Are you all right?"

"I don't follow."

"You talk about your home as if it were trash."

"My home?"

"Yeah, Estrella, do you need me to spell it out for you? This barrio is your home."

"Why are you getting so pissed?"

He stood up, shoved his hands in his pockets, and searched the sky for an explanation. I got up slowly.

"I just hate it when people put down my barrio. You know, there's a reason your homegirl's neighborhood is so clean. Do you know that street sweepers clean some streets on a daily basis? These same city employees come to the East Side once a week. Does that sound fair to you?"

I shook my head. It really *didn't* sound fair. I felt like something else was opening up inside my head.

Speedy took a deep breath to calm his nerves.

"I'm not mad at you, Estrella," he finally said. "I'm mad at the system. I'm mad at this country that says that everyone is equal and then treats some people one way and some people a totally different way. That's all." Speedy looked down at his shoes.

"I'm sorry, too," I said reluctantly. "I'm sorry for going on about my girl's place. You must think I'm a total idiot."

"I do not." He smirked, pulling me close.

It was hard to think of anything when Speedy was standing so close. His sweet cologne was dancing all around me. The tip of his nose softly touched mine and I swallowed hard. I could feel his short, shallow breaths and wondered if he was going to kiss me. Finally! I closed my eyes and puckered my lips, ready for my first kiss.

Then my phone started vibrating out of control. There was a text message from Christie that said: UR MOM CALLED 2X. SHE'S PISSED.

"Damn!" I said. "I gotta go home."

"Yo, let me walk with you."

"You can't. My mother would hit us so hard, we'd have *chancla* marks on our foreheads for a month."

"You exaggerate too much. Your mom loves me."

"Yeah, when you were small, cute, and helpless."

"Hey, I'm still cute," he joked.

"One out of three isn't good enough, especially when you're on the street like a *vago*."

Speedy shook his head. "There you go again, putting your people down. Chilling ain't a bad thing."

"Well, explain that to my dad."

Speedy winced. He was probably thinking about my dad's size and thick arms. "You know, I just remembered that I have this appointment."

"Aha." I smiled. "What a coincidence."

We stopped a few blocks away my house. Somebody was having a party. Twenty cars were triple-parked in front of my neighbor's blue house. There was the familiar scent of a barbecue, the sound of *ranchera* music, and kids screaming at the top of their lungs.

"Well, will you call me again soon?" he asked. But before I could answer, he dashed down the street.

Is Speedy really afraid of my dad? I wondered as I walked home. I stepped carefully on the sidewalk, avoiding all cracks. My mom already had a bad back and I didn't want to make it worse. There were black and orange balloons taped to the railing of the green house on the corner. They must have been leftovers from last Halloween. The house next to it was yellow, but the paint was peeling so badly, you could see it had once been painted gray. Almost all the front lawns had brown patches where the grass had dried up from neglect.

Why did Speedy care so much about this community when the people here couldn't have cared less? All they thought about was living for the next party. Didn't he want to be successful and have stuff that he could be proud of? What was wrong with having a nice car? If I worked hard, didn't I deserve to have nice stuff? But then, how had Speedy been able to make me feel so ashamed earlier? I shook my head, confused. I wasn't even sure what I thought anymore.

entiendes (in-'tyen-dayz) n., Spanish, formal: 1. to understand or "get it." Usually used in the form of a question at the end of a real long speech. It's my dad's favorite ending phrase.

I DIDN'T SEE MY MOM'S CAR IN THE DRIVEWAY when I got home. As for my dad, he was watching a wrestling match with my grandmother. Wrestling and Bud Light were the only two things Dad and Nana had in common. They both got really excited and jumped up and down and would high-five every time one of their favorite wrestlers won a match. Sometimes I'd watch with them, but Nana always got annoyed with me because I couldn't keep track of all the soapy dramas.

"Where have you been?" my dad asked, his jaw twitching. "Your mother and I were worried. She was just about to drive around looking for you, but I convinced her to go ahead without you." He turned his attention back to the TV. "You owe me one, *mija*."

I took a deep breath. *This is* my *life*, I told myself. I was no longer a little girl, and I needed to stand up for myself. "Dad, can we talk?"

"I'm trying to watch the Rock!" Nana said. She hated to be interrupted during her favorite show.

He looked up at me with a curious expression, then back at Nana, who was using a pillow as a punching bag. "In the kitchen," he said.

As I walked into the other room, I felt like I was going to faint. I tried to concentrate on what I wanted to say as my dad slid into a chair. He looked so uncomfortable and big sitting alone at the dwarf-size table. He motioned for me to sit, but I shook my head. I didn't want to lose my nerve.

"Dad, I need to talk to you."

"What's the matter?" he asked with concern.

"I just want you to listen to me, okay? Promise me you won't interrupt."

He took a deep breath, leaned back, and put his hands behind his head. Then he nodded for me to continue.

"Dad, I know you want me to focus on school right now, but I have to tell you, I've been going out with Speedy behind your back."

His eyes bugged out as if he were choking on a piece of chili. "Who?"

"Agapito, from the other day. I know you told me not to, but it's not what you think. He's a good friend and not a bad influence at all. In fact, he's really smart."

"I don't believe this!" he said, smacking the table with his heavy palm. He shot up from his chair like a firework. "You disobeyed me! After all the sacrifices I've made for you, this is how you repay me?" He waved a fist in the air.

"No, Dad, it's not like that!"

"Can't you get it through your head? I don't want you to date. You can date all you want when you get older. But right now you have to stay on top of your work."

"I am, Dad. The lowest grade I got last semester was an A minus."

"Well, you obviously have too much time on your hands if you're sneaking out to be with that boy. Damn it, Estrella, why can't you just listen to me? Have you no respect?"

"I do, Dad."

"I've never been ashamed of you before, but now I see that you're no different from your cousin." He turned away and stared at the oak cabinets with a frustrated look on his face. My parents had sacrificed a lot to help me get that scholarship. I remembered how last year my dad had stopped going to Giants games so that we'd have extra money to buy my school supplies and uniform. Going to Sacred Heart was as much their success as it was mine.

I reached out and put my hand on his shoulder. I looked into Dad's eyes and I could tell I was breaking his heart. *He doesn't deserve this,* I thought. This was a terrible idea, and it left a miserable taste in my mouth. He pulled away from me as if I were a poisonous snake.

"I'm sorry, Dad."

He spun around quickly and caught me off guard. "Obviously, you're not mature enough to know how to follow instructions. Your mother is always on my case about how I give you too much freedom, and now I think she's right."

I was burning with shame.

"I've made up my mind. You're not allowed to date anyone until I say so." He looked toward the door. "And you can forget about staying over at your friend's house. You're grounded. *Entiendes?*"

I walked to my room and closed the door. I sat down on the yellow animal-print bedspread. I balled my hands into fists and punched my pillow. It didn't make me feel better.

Ten minutes later, Mom made me come out into the living room and then lectured me for an hour about responsibility, just for being late! I thought that Dad might say something about Speedy, but he was so annoyed by Mom's speech that he went out back without dinner. I felt horrible about what I'd told him and wanted him to forgive me. But every time I tried to approach him, I lost my nerve.

I knew my friends wouldn't understand, so I didn't even bother trying to explain. At school, Christie and Sheila could only talk about the upcoming party. How much fun it was going to be, who would be there, what they were going to wear, what other people might be wearing, what music they'd play. And on and on and on. I had to remind myself that this was *my* birthday party they were talking about. *My party!* I should have been excited, but I couldn't help feeling totally left out of planning this event, too.

And then, back at my house, things were no better. Like

clockwork, my dad called my mom every afternoon at four o'clock to make sure that I was home. I tried to be as agreeable as possible, praying that he would lift my punishment before Christie's party. I knew that I shouldn't see Speedy ever again. I didn't want to hurt my father any more. So I didn't call him, but I missed him terribly.

Then, on Friday, as I was leaving school with Christie and Sheila, I noticed Speedy waiting across the street.

Without a second thought, I dashed over to him. "What are you doing here?" I'd been thinking about him almost constantly for the past couple of days. I could hardly believe he was standing there in front of me. I felt dizzy.

"I had to see you," he said. "You never called me." He looked hurt.

"I know. I'm so sorry. But you'll never believe what happened! I told my dad about you. And I felt really good about that . . . until he totally flipped out and said I was way too young to date."

"This is all my fault," Speedy said, looking over my shoulder. "I'm sorry for showing up unannounced. But I just had to talk to you."

I wanted to rush into his arms and give him a big hug. But then I became uncomfortably aware that we were under public scrutiny. I turned and saw Christie and Sheila walking toward us. I waved casually at them. What was I going to do? I could already imagine how Sheila and Christie would look at him, what they'd think about him. Or even worse, what they might say. I leaned over and whispered to Speedy, "I think you should go."

But it was too late.

"Hey, Star," Sheila said as she sauntered over. "Who's your friend?" She raised one eyebrow.

Christie came up beside her and looked curiously at Speedy.

"Um . . . this is a friend of my brother's," I said quickly. Speedy looked at me, confused.

Sheila waved halfheartedly.

There was an awkward pause. Sheila crossed her arms and said nothing. This was a mistake.

Christie stretched out her hand. "Nice to meet you."

"Um, he was just leaving," I said, pushing Speedy away. "I'll explain later," I whispered into his ear.

Speedy gave me an annoyed look.

"Come on, guys," I said to Sheila and Christie. I turned to Speedy as I was pulling them away. "Well, thanks for stopping by." When we were safely across the street, I caught sight of Speedy turning the corner on his bike. Part of me wanted to chase after him. A big part.

"Okay, Star," Sheila said impatiently. "He's gone. Now tell us who he really is."

"Yeah," Christie jumped in. "Is that the boy you told us about?" I nodded.

"He looks like a thug," Sheila said.

"Yeah. Not really my type." Christie shook her head. "I don't like bad boys."

"You're such a liar!" Sheila shrieked, slapping her on the arm.

"Okay, unless he has a body like Usher's," Christie said.

I wanted to joke with my friends and tried to put on an amused smile. But my heart ached. I wanted to defend Speedy. I hated to pretend that he was just another guy.

Christie grabbed my arm. "Star, what about Kevin?"

"What *about* Kevin?"

"I thought you said you liked him."

"I liked talking to him on the phone that one time. Why?"

Christie started chewing on her lower lip. She did this when-ever she was frustrated. I'd seen that look countless times before while we were studying for finals. "Mark and Kevin are on their way over right now. Kevin made me promise not to tell you. It was going to be a surprise."

"You're kidding, right? Why would you do that?" I asked. I felt my face growing hot. I knew my voice was coming out more angry-sounding than I meant it to.

Christie just blushed. "Kevin thought it would be fun to play pool at my house before the party started. I don't know why you're making such a big deal about it."

Right, the party.

Now I had to find a way to sneak out of the house and get over to Christie's *and* find the time to apologize to Speedy. I also had to do it without my parents knowing, and given the brand-new tiny leash they had me on, that was going to be very, very tricky.

"Sorry guys," I said. "I just can't do that right now. I'll see you tonight."

As I walked away, my heart was pounding. Would Christie and Sheila be mad at me for leaving? Should I go back and hang out with them? And what about Speedy? Was he going to be mad at me, too? I forced my feet to keep moving, but I really had no idea where I wanted to go.

THIS IS ALMOST TOO EASY, I thought as I climbed out of my bedroom window with the straps of a pair of spike heels clenched between my teeth. The house was still. There wasn't even a breeze on this surprisingly warm night. I raced down the street barefoot to catch the 12:15 A.M. bus across town.

There was a group of guys loitering in front of the bus stop. They were typical hood rats who liked to crack jokes, mock fight, and drink from paper bags. I felt a little uneasy as I walked by, because I knew they were going to say something. Good girls didn't walk around my neighborhood alone at this hour.

"*Ay, mamacita,*" a skinny guy with a buzz cut howled over the other catcalls. "Check out them legs!" I ignored them, keeping a good ten feet between us. *Idiot,* I thought to myself, but I had to admit, the dress Christie had given me made me look hot. It was tight at the waist and full around the hips, showing off an hourglass figure I had no idea I had. The white heels made my legs appear long and slender.

I kept walking. *Where is the goddamn bus?* I cursed to myself, pulling my thin coat even tighter around my body. The coat made me feel exposed. I felt like these punks were imagining me naked underneath it. I bounced up and down on my toes. I could run if I had to, but not in these shoes. *Come on, bus,* I thought to myself. *Hurry up!*

"Leave her alone," a familiar voice said. I turned around and there was Speedy. "She's with me." Speedy's crew responded with a series of heckles and pounded on his shoulders in congratulation.

"Yeah, Speedy!"

"Speedy's a pimp, got a way with the la-dies."

"She's hot," hollered a chubby boy with no neck. "She got any sisters?"

"Shut up, man," Speedy said harshly. He walked over to me slowly as if testing the waters. "Hey, what's up?"

I couldn't believe Speedy was being so nice to me, especially after the way I'd dissed him in front of my friends. I had to explain. "You know Speedy, about what happened—"

"I already forgot about it," he said, sounding tense.

"Will you let me explain?"

"What for? So that you can tell me that you're embarrassed to introduce me to your friends?"

"It's not like that," I said softly.

"Then what is it?"

But I didn't have an answer. Speedy sighed, as if he were trying to be patient with a little child. He started to check out my heels and asked, "You going to a party?"

"I'm going to Christie's. You met her. She's the really pretty girl with the long blond hair."

He nodded and motioned to his boys. "That's cool. We're looking for a party. Can we tag along?"

"No, don't say anything," I shushed him, worrying that his gangster friends would follow me and destroy everything. "It's not that kind of party."

He looked at me blankly.

"It's invitation-only," I lied.

I saw Speedy's jaw muscles twitch. He spat on the ground. "Okay, that's cool. You wanna be like that. Go to your fancy party with your rich-ass white friends. I'm sure everyone will be driving Beemers or Hummers and showing off some brand-new threads that they paid five hundred dollars for." He looked at my coat, and then he looked me straight in the eye. "Stop with the games, all right? I ain't no fool. Why don't you try being straight up for once? The truth is that you'd be embarrassed to be seen with me and my boys. You think we're not good enough for your party," he said flatly. "And you think I'm not good enough for you."

"No, it's not like that. *I'm* not like that." But *was* it like that? What was I *doing*? What was I afraid of?

"Oh, you don't think so? Well, then, what the hell *are* you like? Maybe you should take a better look in the mirror and figure it out."

I opened my mouth and then snapped it shut.

"You got issues," he said in a low voice so the others wouldn't hear. Maybe he didn't want to embarrass me. "Why do you care so much about what other people think? People who'll judge you by how you look or where you're from are not your peeps. You don't need people like that." He waited for me to say something, but I didn't. "Whatever. We don't want to go to your party. Who wants to be around a *vendida* anyway?"

Just then, the bus pulled up and screeched to a stop. The door swung open and the driver waited for me to get on. I had no idea what to say, so I just stepped onto the bus and the doors closed behind me. Speedy's friends started yelling after the bus while he stood there staring at his feet. Tears welled up in my eyes as the bus rolled along and they disappeared into the night. *I didn't have a choice,* I told myself. *I am . . .*

I wiped my eyes and looked up. There was Izzy, watching me from the back of the bus. I knew that it was about to get worse. Izzy had colored her hair Christmas tree green. The nose ring was gone, but instead she had a hoop in her lip. She was wearing a rhinestone tee that said *Meow* (in black, her favorite color) and low-cut jeans that showed off a butterfly tattoo around her navel.

"Hey, stranger," she said when I sat down. We made eye contact. Her face softened. "What's wrong?"

I wanted to talk to someone, someone who might understand.

"Remember Agapito from fourth grade?" I started. "Well I've been kinda seein' him. It's not like when we were kids and fighting all the time. Wait a sec. Who am I kiddin'? I'm crazy about the boy. I don't know how it happened; it just did. We've been hanging out all the time. It's so cool, 'cause I can tell him everything and he totally gets me. But . . . I was on my way to my friend Christie's party and he wanted to bring all his thug friends along. And I just felt weird, 'cause I didn't want to bring a bunch of *cholos* to crash the party. It's just plain rude, so I said he shouldn't come, y'know? And now he's all mad at me." I looked down at my dress. "But I don't think it's fair." I wanted Izzy to tell me that Speedy was a *cholo* and that I'd done the right thing by leaving him behind.

"That's not cool, Estrella," Izzy said after a minute. "Don't give me this "it's rude" bullshit. It's obvious what you're doing: you're dumping him like you dumped me and Tere."

"That's not true at all!"

Izzy stared at me for a long time as if she were considering my words. "What is it with you?" she said quietly.

"You don't understand. My parents don't want me to see him either."

Izzy gave me the cold shoulder. "Don't blame your parents for your actions. Why don't you ever take any responsibility?" Izzy said between clenched teeth.

I looked down at my feet and said nothing.

"Have fun at your party." Izzy stood up and rang the bell. She got off the bus, leaving me to think about what she'd said and what I'd done.

tequila (tay-'kee-lah) n., Spanish, formal: 1. an alcoholic drink that comes from Mexico 2. made from a cactus plant called agave 3. They always have bottles of it at family parties. I'm not allowed to touch the stuff.

As I WALKED ALONE ON THE SIDEWALK, dark shadows loomed from lampposts, and twisted bushes tricked my eyes into seeing things that weren't there. I knew in a few minutes I'd be surrounded by people, but right then I felt totally alone.

At night, Christie's neighborhood lost all its charm. It reminded me of some scary horror flick, where insane lunatics chased babysitters across front lawns. I'd always thought it was funny how all the maniac killers usually turned up in rich white neighborhoods. I wondered what the *cholos* would do if a crazy killer came into our barrio. They'd probably jump him and teach him a lesson.

Soon enough, I came upon Christie's house. Shiny new SUVs, sports cars, and a bright yellow Hummer were parked out front. I tried to imagine what Speedy and his friends might think if they were there with me. I bit my lip and swallowed hard. I tried to shake the thoughts out of my head. I could hear Omarion's latest hit blasting as I approached the door.

"Hello? Who's there?" Christie asked from the other end of the intercom.

"It's me, Star."

"Star!" Christie sounded relieved. "It's about time. Just a minute." She buzzed me in.

Sheila swung open the front door with Christie right behind her. Sheila looked hot, standing under the glow of the doorway pillars. She wore a pink Kangol hat, a tube top, white silk capris, and matching stiletto heels. Her dark hair was feathered out in a seventies-style cut.

"Finally! I thought you weren't coming." Christie pouted. She looked like she was ready to dance backup in a Beyoncé video. She was wearing a pair of bootylicious baby-blue shorts that showed off her extra-long legs, a white baby tee, and platform heels. She'd braided her strawberry blond hair tight; the braids had cute blue bows on the ends. (Move over, Dorothy!)

Sheila closed the door behind her. "I was worried your parents might not let you out."

"Oh my God, Star!" Christie cried when I came into the light. "You look fabulous. I love that dress."

"Thank you, dahling," I said in a sophisticated prima donna accent. I forced myself to smile.

"Oh, those poor fools," Sheila said with a smile. "They have no idea how lucky they are to have three of the most beautiful girls at their fingertips."

We walked into the living room, which was already crowded. I felt uncomfortable and excited all at the same time. *Here I am!* I thought to myself. *I snuck out and now I'm at a party!* It almost didn't feel real. I recognized some of the girls from school and a couple of boys from Christie's birthday back in January. But the majority of people I'd never seen before. There were more than a couple of beefy boys with Caesar cuts getting their groove on out on the dance floor.

I turned the corners of my mouth up into a smile. *This was fun, right? Yes. Definitely. This was going to be fun.*

Most of the valuable paintings and big chunky pieces had been moved out of the room, leaving a huge dance space, and two leather love seats stood alongside the dramatic stairs leading to the second floor. The steam from perspiring dancers fogged up the glass windows that overlooked Christie's swimming pool and stone-lined spa. There was a giant plasma-screen TV on the wall. A makeshift bar had been set up and was covered with a dozen different bottles of liquor, everything from Grey Goose vodka to Tanqueray gin. There were even a few bottles of fancy Veuve Clicquot champagne.

One day, I told myself, *I'll have all this, too.* I imagined what Speedy might have said if he were here with me. Maybe he'd just have shaken his head. *There's nothing wrong with wanting it,* I said to the imaginary Speedy. *Anyone would.*

We were standing in the foyer that led into the living room. This was our dramatic entrance, so we paused. Everyone could see us from here.

"Who wants a drink?" Sheila asked as she elbowed her way to the bar in the corner.

"I'll be right with you," Christie said and disappeared into the crowd.

"Are you playing bartender?" I leaned against the counter to face the dance floor and check out the scene. I was sure that almost all the guys went to Saint Ignatius or some other prep school. They all had this "I know I'm all that" attitude, which Sheila and Christie found so attractive and had been trying to teach me to like. I glanced over my shoulder, and Sheila gave me a crooked smile as she carefully placed four tiny glasses on the counter.

"I thought we'd need a little something to get this party started," Sheila said.

"Four glasses?"

She leaned over the counter, exposing more of herself than I cared to see. I worried that she might fall out of her top if she didn't watch out. A few guys in the corner also seemed to be noticing this, but they didn't seem too concerned. Neither did Sheila.

"Well, you never know when a certain really hot guy might show up," she said.

I didn't know what to say. I felt my stomach tighten. The only really hot guy I wanted to see was Speedy. Tears sprang to my eyes, but I blinked them back. Thanks to me, there was zero chance he'd be at this party.

"Be cool, here he comes. . . ."

"Hey, you got enough for me?" a deep, full voice said from behind me. I turned around and looked into Kevin McDonough's beautiful hazel eyes. He had big broad shoulders and a strong athletic build underneath his button-down black shirt and khaki pants. His clothes hugged his frame. I thought of Speedy in his giant khaki pants.

Christie, who was standing right behind Kevin, popped out with a big grin on her face. "Oh Staa-ar, I brought you a little present." She winked at me. I tried to smile back, but it made my face hurt.

"All right, guys," Sheila announced, "Who's first?" She was holding a bottle of Jose Cuervo in her hand like it was a priceless jewel.

"That stuff's nasty." Christie made a disgusted face. "I don't know how you can drink it."

"It's not that bad," Sheila argued. "It's a pretty good tequila. Right, Star?"

Sheila wanted me to back her up. As if being Mexican meant I knew everything about tequila.

"I've actually never tried it," I said quietly.

"It's nasty," Christie repeated, sticking her tongue out.

"No, it's not," Kevin said. "You just got to know how to drink it."

Sheila giggled. "Kevin, I like how you think!" She poured him an inch of alcohol.

"Here," he said, handing her a second glass. "Pour one for Star." He gave me a wink. "I'm sure she can handle it."

"No, thanks," I said. "I don't drink."

"Oh come on," Kevin insisted, "It's a party. *Relaaaaaax*," he said. "Have a little fun."

There was a tightness in my chest. *Relax.* I hadn't been truly relaxed in such a long time. *This is what you've always wanted!* I told myself. *Here you are in this beautiful house with your cool friends about to have a drink with a very hot guy. This is what you wanted!* "All right," I said, grabbing the shot glass. "Lead the way."

Kevin grabbed a slice of lemon from the bar and licked the back of his hand. "Now, all you have to remember is lick, drink, suck."

"Lick, drink, suck," I repeated.

"Yeah, it's easy." He smiled. "Now watch." He sprinkled salt on his hand. "Lick." He licked the salt off his hand. "Drink." He swallowed the entire glass of tequila. "And suck." He bit into the lemon slice and winced. "Your turn."

I licked my hand and sprinkled it with salt. "I lick," I said as I licked off the salt. "Then I drink. . . ." The minute I smelled the tequila, my stomach began to churn. I tried to drink the entire shot, but I began to choke. My eyes started to water. I felt like I was going to throw up.

"You can't sip it or it'll make you sick." Kevin laughed. "You got to drink it all at once."

"This stuff *is* nasty."

"Oh, come on, Star," Sheila griped. "Let's all do it together."

Christie lifted an empty shot glass in a determined pose. "I guess I'll do it, too."

"All for one and one for all," I said. It came out sounding sarcastic. I hoped no one would notice.

Kevin filled up our glasses.

"All right, on the count of three," I said. "One, two, three." We licked, drank, and sucked. The tequila burned my throat and warmed my stomach. There was a surge of energy that came with the disgusting taste. The tightness in my chest started to melt.

"How about another round?" I said, trying to act excited. I wanted to show them what a good time I was having, how much fun I could be.

Christie shook her head. "I'm done. I have no tolerance for that stuff." She walked off into the crowd of dancers.

"I should go too," Sheila said as she sashayed over to a group of guys huddled in the corner. In no time at all, Sheila was the focus of the group. The boys were acting stupid and elbowing each other out of the way, competing for her attention.

My girls were ditching me—they were obviously trying to give me some time alone with Kevin. But I wasn't sure I *wanted* to be alone with him. Whatever. It was too late. I turned around and Kevin was already filling up our glasses again.

"So, Star," Kevin said. "What kind of name is that? Indian?"

"Actually, my name is Estrella."

"Es-tray-ah. That's different. I don't think I've ever met anyone with that name."

"It's Spanish for Star," I said flatly.

"It's pretty." He smiled. "Like your dress." He looked me up and down, his eyes lingering on my plunging neckline. The tip of his tongue came out of his mouth, and was I imagining it, or did he just lick his lips ever so slightly? He stepped a little closer and I could smell his cologne. It smelled like the men's section of a department store.

"Thanks," I said, feeling tense. The eager look in his eyes reminded me of the horny *cholos* from my neighborhood. I took a step back.

"Ready for another round?" Kevin asked.

I looked over at Sheila, who was sexing it up on the dance floor. She mouthed, "Go for it."

I missed Speedy, but this party was what I'd been so excited about. If I didn't even get myself to have fun, then what was the point? What was the point of *any* of it?

The second round went a lot smoother than the first.

My whole body felt looser, and my face was tingling just a little.

"I'm glad you came," Kevin said when we finished. "At first I didn't think you'd show up."

"I got held up on the bus."

"You took the bus? I wish I would've known. I would have given you a ride."

"I live pretty far."

"How far?"

"Close to the East Side."

He shrugged. "That's not too far."

I smiled. Maybe this night would turn out okay after all.

After another shot, Kevin wanted to dance.

"C'mon, Star," he coaxed while pulling me onto the dance floor. "I know your type. You like to pretend to be shy, but you're really wild on the inside."

I looked around and saw Christie with a beer in one hand and her other hand on Mark's chest. Their hips were wedged together and they were gyrating to Sean Paul's "Shake That Thing." They were staring intensely at each other like they were the only people there.

Did he expect me to do *that?*

Kevin pulled me close—so close, I could tell his minty-fresh gum was still working. We hardly knew each other and we were in a tight embrace. I could feel his breath on my neck. I didn't know what to do, so I kind of just hung there like a rag doll.

"You're so hot," Kevin whispered. "And such a *sweet girl*. Your friends were so right about what they said about you." He started kissing my neck in a way that I could only assume was supposed to be sexy. But it was just all slobbery—like a Saint Bernard was licking me hello.

I sort of tried to squirm away, but he didn't seem to notice. He just held me tighter.

I closed my eyes, but my mind was solely on Speedy. Even though Kevin was the ultimate in guys and Sheila and Christie thought he'd be perfect for me, there was only one person who truly made me feel alive and special and comfortable in my own skin—Speedy. I felt this weird, cold truth come over me. I'd sold him out tonight, and now I was dancing with my reward.

My eyes shot open the second Kevin's hands started

wandering up and down my body. I pushed my hands against his chest, trying to back up. But he wouldn't let me go.

"What are you doing, Star?" Kevin murmured into my ear. "You don't need to do this pretend playing-hard-to-get stuff. Your friends already told me you were into it."

Then he breathed in deep, like he was trying to inhale me. And before I even had time to protest, something happened. I should have been expecting it, I guess, but for some reason it still surprised me. He reached down and grabbed my ass.

What I did next was like a gut reaction, an instinct. And if Speedy had been there watching, he would've been proud.

I reached up and slapped Kevin right across his stupid, slimy face. Really, *really* hard.

"What the fuck!?" Kevin said. His cheek turned bright pink.

"Like you said, I'm wild on the inside!" I yelled. And with that I turned on my heel and stormed into the closest bathroom. Christie's house had like ten of them, and each one had its own theme. This bathroom was decorated in soft peach colors and had a citrusy smell. As soon as I slammed the door behind me, I started crying. It felt like everything that had happened in the past couple weeks was piled up on top of my head. It was crushing me. Tears were rolling down my face.

There was a knock on the door.

"Star," Sheila yelled. "It's me and Christie. Will you let us in?"

I opened the door and pulled them inside.

"I've had it!" I shouted.

Christie and Sheila looked at me, surprised. Christie plopped down on the toilet. She looked peeved. "Well, I don't know what your problem is," she slurred. "I'm having a great time. Then Sheila grabs me out of Mark's arms like there's some huge emergency."

Sheila leaned back against the counter. "What the hell happened? I thought you were getting along with Kevin. Then I hear you slapped him in front of everyone."

"You did!" Christie said. "How could you do that? Now you totally blew it with him!"

"Seriously, Star," Sheila said, crossing her arms. "That's really ungrateful of you. Christie really put a lot of time into this, saying nice things about you and whatever."

"He was all over me!" I exploded.

Sheila gave me a naughty smile. "Star, don't play innocent with me. I saw you two on the dance floor."

I shook my head. "Kevin is a punk. He was slobbering all over me and when I tried to push him off, he wouldn't let go! Then he said that *you* told him I'd be into it. And then he grabbed my ass! What did you expect me to do?"

"Don't be such a prude, Star," Christie huffed. "All guys do that. You can't go around slapping every guy who grabs your ass."

"And why not?" I asked.

"Because, because . . ." Christie got all flustered and looked at Sheila for help.

"Because people will think you're an icy cold bitch," Sheila said. "Damn it, Star, do we have to explain everything to you?" She laid her hands on my shoulders. "I'm sure he's over there right now telling everybody all kinds of shit about you!"

I shrugged her off. "Well, I don't care."

"You *will* care when no one wants to date you," Christie mumbled.

I couldn't believe what they were saying.

"Didn't you hear me? I said I was fed up. I'm tired of you telling me what to think and who to date or how to act just so I that can be more like you."

"We're just trying to help, Star," Christie said. "We're just trying to help make you happy."

"Well, you know what? Being more like *you* isn't going to make me happy. I used to think it would. But I never *was* quite happy, all this time! I busted my ass trying to do everything you guys did and trying to go along with everything you said just to be more like you. But that was a big mistake. It's one I won't make again."

Sheila threw her hands up. "I can't believe I'm hearing this. I need a cigarette." She pulled out a pack from her back pocket and lit one up.

"Not in the house," Christie whined.

"Give it a rest, Chris," Sheila snapped. She opened the window and blew a puff of smoke outside.

Christie turned back to me, angrily. She looked as if she wanted to rearrange my face.

"And another thing: I don't even like Kevin," I said. "Yeah, so he has a nice face and an Abercrombie body, but so what? He's still kind of an asshole. And even if he weren't, it wouldn't matter. I love Speedy." I was surprised to hear myself say it, but as the words came out of my mouth, I knew they were true.

"Wait, are you talking about that thuggy boy who came to the school the other day?" Sheila asked.

"He's not in your league, Star." Christie was trying hard to talk me out of it.

"You don't even know Speedy," I blurted out.

"Fine, so we don't *know him* know him," Christie said. "But we saw him, and we know his type. You could do so much better."

"Speedy isn't a *type*. He's an actual person, a *real* person," I said, stomping my foot. "He's smart, funny, and very sweet. He wouldn't try and grab the ass of some girl he barely even knows."

Sheila looked at me and shook her head like I was a small child throwing a tantrum. "Star, you're really losing it here. You don't know a thing about guys. Why are you wasting your time with him when you have an amazing guy right here who'd be totally perfect for you?"

Christie added, "Maybe if you really apologize and just tell him you were drunk or something, then Kevin will understand."

"You're not listening to a word I'm saying," I said. "*I am not interested in Kevin.* Speedy cares about me as a person, the actual me, not some fake-ass, dressed-up-in-someone-else's-clothes, drunk version of me. Kevin is a jerk, and if you think he's so perfect for me, maybe you *don't* know me at all. Speedy doesn't pity me the way you guys do, and Speedy doesn't try and turn me into something I'm not. Speedy understands where I come from, because he comes from there, too." I took a deep breath. "He knows me better than you guys ever could."

Sheila and Christie stared at me dumbfounded. Their silence was killing me. I had to get some fresh air and quick, or I was going to be sick. Just as the *quince* was part of my parents' plan for me, Kevin had been part of *their* plan for me. Regardless of what I had to say or what I thought, they thought they knew better. But I was sick of it.

It was time for me to make my own plans.

"I'm out of here," I said, stumbling toward the door.

"Star," Christie said. She reached out and tried to grab my hand.

"This is so nuts," Sheila said.

"Know what I think is so nuts?" I said, brushing Christie's hand away. "I think it's so nuts that I ever wanted to be like you. And I think it's so nuts that I ever thought we were friends."

Then I grabbed my coat and stormed out of the house. But as I was leaving, a thought came to me: soft clay is easy to mold, but if you're strong and solid deep in your core, then no one can touch you. No matter how much someone might possibly try to change you, it only works if you let them. I crossed my arms and squared my shoulders. I set off down the pretty street, headed right back the way I'd come.

★ *19* ★

> **confianza** (kon-fee-'ahn-zah) v., Spanish, formal: 1. to trust. It's when you feel super-comfortable with someone. You can tell that person anything and know that she/he will not backstab you in any way.

I KEPT WALKING DOWN THE DARK SIDEWALK, but really, I had no idea where I was going. The buses were no longer running and I had no money for a cab. I couldn't call my brothers. That would have awoken everyone at home. I certainly couldn't call Speedy.

Just when I thought things couldn't get any worse, I felt something nasty stir in my stomach. I drew in a deep breath of air and immediately threw up all over someone's landscaped bushes. I fell on my knees in the grass.

I was in deep shit and I had no idea what to do.

I thought about calling Marta. Marta had always looked out for me. I remembered the time I'd been caught eating mean old Mr. Uribe's figs. He'd warned me to stay away from his tree, but I just hadn't been able to resist the delicious figs hanging there. When he caught me in his yard for the third time, I was sure he was going to tell my parents and I'd be dead. But Marta had come to the rescue. She'd knocked on Mister Uribe's door and ten minutes later, not only was I out of trouble, but he'd given me a basket of figs to take home, too. I smiled, thinking of my cousin. I hadn't called her in a long time. There was no other option but to swallow my pride. She was the only one who could bail me out.

I pulled out the cell Sheila had given me and dialed her number.

"Hello?"

"Marta?"

"Estrella, what a *sorpresa!*" Marta said cheerfully. Then her voice grew serious. "Is my mother all right?"

"Yeah, she's fine. I didn't mean to worry you. I'm sorry for calling so late."

"No prob. I was up anyway, studying for a final."

"I need a huge favor."

"Tell me," Marta said with *confianza.*

"Could you come get me?"

Marta started to laugh. It was so loud, I had to pull my ear from the phone.

"Are you locked up?" she finally asked.

"No!"

Marta chuckled again. "Just checking. So where are you at?"

Less than twenty minutes later, Marta was helping me into her beat-up Geo. Her babies were asleep in the backseat. "You'll be fine," she told me as I strapped myself in. "Nothing a good bowl of *menudo* can't cure. You okay?"

I just nodded.

"Just let me know if you're feeling sick and I'll pull over to the side of the road."

I nodded, hoping there was nothing left in my stomach. Marta was so cool. She didn't ask for any explanations. My eyelids grew heavy and began to close. I didn't wake up until the car's engine turned off. We were parked in front of a simple two-story apartment complex off a busy intersection. A car whizzed by at lightning speed, setting off about a dozen car alarms at the same time. How did Marta stand all the noise? Marta carried Maya into the ground-floor apartment. Temo continued to sleep in his car seat with his head leaning on the window.

Marta walked back to the car. "Let's go," she said, opening my door.

I watched as she carefully pulled the sleeping child from the car. Marta was wearing a pair of baggy gray sweats and a *Cinco de Mayo* T-shirt. Her long black hair was tightly woven into a thick braid down her back.

Seeing the long braid reminded me of the time *Tía* Lucky had said that Marta had joined some kind of Indian cult. My *tía* had come into our house in hysterics, claiming that God was punishing her for something she'd done in a past life. Apparently, she'd seen Marta dancing at an Avon convention with feathers in her hair and prancing around like a hippie. I wondered how much of that was really true. Marta was always interested in learning about our Mexican roots and had a lot of pride in her dark skin and her flat Indian butt. I remembered all the books she had brought over and the time she'd taken me to the Aztec dance class at the rec center.

I looked around her apartment. There were posters of Indian warriors carrying scantily clothed women and a *taquería* calendar with mountain landscapes. A huge black Aztec calendar hung above her leather couch. A colorful serape covered a coffee table in the center of the room, and an altar, much like Nana's, with candles and pictures of the Virgin Mary was in the corner.

Marta came out of one of the adjoining bedrooms. She looked like she hadn't slept since she had Temo.

"Have a seat, hon." Her voice sounded so much like that of my *tía*, who had been raised in south Texas.

When Marta had gotten pregnant, *Tía* Lucky had thrown a fit. "What will the neighbors say?" she'd complained. I remembered the last time I'd seen the two of them speak to each other. Or rather, yell at each other. It was more than four years ago, right after Marta got pregnant and before she moved out. We were having a barbecue in my parent's backyard and the air was thick with smoke. *Tía* was really laying into Marta something terrible. "You are a disgrace to our family," *Tía* had said to her. "I tried to steer you in the right direction, but all the decisions you've made have been the wrong ones, you stupid, stupid girl." I remembered the look on Marta's face when her mother said that. Her eyes had flashed with anger, but then the anger had turned to sadness. She'd pressed her lips tightly together, and she hadn't said anything.

Now Marta was standing in front of the stove. Her kitchen was painted bright pink. The room was bare except for a round table, three mismatched chairs, and a Fisher-Price child's easel in the corner. But it felt like home, with the warm scent of tortillas in the air.

"Do you want some water?" she asked.

"Yes, please."

She glanced at my outfit. "So how was the party?"

"It was all right," I said, taking the glass she offered.

"You're lucky I was studying for a final or else you would have been out of luck." She turned off the electric stove and served me a bowl of *menudo*.

"When did you go back to school?" I asked. *Tía* had told me Marta had dropped out of high school and was hanging out with a bunch of *cholas*.

"I never really left." She chuckled, as if she knew what I was thinking. "But this is my first year of dental school, so I want to do well. Here, eat some of this and you'll feel better."

"Are you studying to be a hygienist?" I asked.

"No, *loca*." She laughed. "To be a dentist!"

A dentist? My parents had given me the impression that Marta's life was total crap and that there was no hope for anyone who dropped out of school. But she was doing fine. She was just the same old Marta I'd known when I was little. She was tougher around the edges but still striving to make something of herself.

Marta put the steaming bowl in front of me. *Menudo* was my favorite. I took a moment and breathed in the delicious aroma of hominy, cilantro, onions, and tripe. Dad called *menudo* a wonder drug. It cured everything from hangovers to home-sickness. The minute I put a spoonful into my mouth, I started to feel better.

Marta watched me silently from across the table. I finished the entire bowl in minutes. She laughed out loud. I'd always loved how Marta laughed with her entire body, and she was never embarrassed by the loudness of it at all. I admired that about her.

"I guess you like my canned *menudo*," she said. "I'll get you another bowl. So what were you drinking tonight?"

"Tequila."

"Ta-kill-ya is what they should call that stuff."

Just then, I realized how much I had missed her, and I wanted to hug her real tight so I wouldn't lose her again.

After she served me another bowl, she asked, "Now, are you going to be straight with me and tell me what's up?"

"What do you mean?"

Marta leaned forward and looked me in the eyes. "You know exactly what I mean. I don't hear from you in months, then all of a sudden you call when you're all trashed."

I shrugged. "I don't know."

"You don't know?" she said, raising her voice in disbelief.

I got real quiet and started fingering the plastic tablecloth nervously. I felt worse than confused. I was overwhelmed with trying to please everyone all the time, and I was always falling short. Now everyone I cared about was upset with me, and I had no idea how to fix any of it. Marta stared at me for a second. She flicked her nails together as if she were restless.

"So, what's going on, *muñeca*?"

"It's nothing."

Marta reached out across the table for my hand. "Come on, Estrella." She looked me straight in the eye. "You can tell me."

Could I? There was so much bottled up, I felt like I would burst.

"My life is a total mess, and I don't know what to do," I blurted out. "Mom and *Tía* are out of control. They're planning this *quince* from hell. The *damas* hate my guts. I have no friends! Oh, and the boy I'm in love with probably won't ever speak to me again."

Marta started laughing.

"What's so funny?"

"Oh, I'm not laughing at you." She giggled. "You got it rough. I'm sure you have your mom, my mom, and Nana teaming up on you." She paused, looking out the kitchen window. "I thought they'd never do another one after the mess I caused."

"But Mom and *Tía* are *obsessed* with your *quince*. 'In Marta's *quince* this, in Marta's *quince* that.' They're driving me crazy!"

"They're crazy, not you." She laughed. "You should have seen the fights I had with my mom. I remember counting once. I think we had twenty-seven fights the week before the party! Remember my dress?"

"Yes."

"That nasty tangerine tent." Marta crinkled her nose as if she were changing Temo's diaper. "I looked like a beach ball. I hated it."

"Guess what? They're making me wear it!"

"No wonder you drink," she joked. "I considered running away, but then I would never have met Suave." She sighed, with a smile on her face. "Who would have known?"

"*Tía* drove you into his arms," I said.

"Well, it wasn't quite like that." She chuckled. "Suave was the DJ at my *quince*."

"Oh?"

"I thought my *quince* would be the worst day of my entire life, but it turned out to be the best. I met the man of my dreams. Oh, don't get me wrong. I did plan to sabotage her party. I ate like a horse for two months, hoping that the dress wouldn't fit. Then I canceled the mariachi band and flower arrangements, just to make her look bad. I was such a bitch." She smiled and then looked at me lovingly. "You were just a little kid then. Now look at you, all grown up, having your own *quince* drama."

"So you can see why I snuck out of my house."

"Yeah, I guess. But what does that solve? You get drunk. Have fun. But tomorrow you'll still have the same problems, no?"

"Well . . ."

"Estrella, don't do what I did. I was too scared to confront my mom. But look at me now. My kids are getting big and my own mother won't come to my son's birthday. I have a good life, and I am happy, but I will always feel that something is missing."

I looked into my cousin's eyes. They were bright but sad. She *hadn't* done badly for herself. I saw her GED hanging on the wall next to mall portraits of her kids and snapshots of our family. Her place was small but cozy. She had truly made a home for herself, but her mother had never set foot inside! What could keep a mother away from her own daughter and her own grand-children?

Our family didn't want Marta around for a terrible, stupid, and superficial reason. There was nothing *wrong* with the way she was living: she just didn't happen to fit into the "perfect family" image they'd all created in their heads. They thought she'd make them look bad. But bad to *who*? Whose opinion mattered so much that it was worth it to desert your own flesh and blood? How could someone so readily forget what really mattered?

I suddenly felt a deep sense of shame gnawing in my gut. I *knew* how someone could forget. It was easy. I'd done it myself.

Without thinking, I got up and gave Marta a hug.

She hugged me and whispered, "Families are supposed to stick together."

"But what do I do?"

"You learn, *chamaca*. Learn from my story and remember you're not alone. If you're honest with the people who love you, maybe they will understand. At least you have to give them the chance. You owe them that much."

"I'm scared."

"Isn't it ironic?" Marta said with a smirk.

"Huh?"

"*La quinceañera* is supposed to mark a woman's transition into womanhood. It's the time when we stop being little girls. But our family doesn't want us to grow up. The bottom line is that they're just as scared as we are. They're scared that we'll grow up and not need them." She started to chuckle to herself. "Our family's so dramatic. Someone should write a *telenovela* about us."

"But Marta . . ." I interrupted. I still didn't understand how that information could help me.

Just then, Suave walked in wearing his security guard uniform. Marta smiled. "Mario works two jobs to help me through school. It's rough."

I didn't remember ever meeting him before. I'd never known he had a real name. Until now, Suave had been a phantom who had come in the night and kidnapped my cousin from her family. Mario was a husky guy with slicked-back hair. He took off his jacket and came to the table. Then he put his arm around Marta's shoulder and leaned down to kiss her on the cheek. She closed her eyes, reached back, and ruffled his hair. He'd closed his eyes, too. And he was smiling.

A second later they both opened their eyes and Mario sat down across from me. Seeing him now, with a tired face and eyes red from lack of sleep, he didn't seem like a cursed man like my *tía* had said.

He smiled weakly and shook my hand. "Hi there."

"You haven't met Mario before?"

I shook my head.

He wiped his eyes and groaned. "I got to be up at seven. Somebody called in sick."

Marta sighed. She turned to Mario and their eyes locked.

"I'm sorry, baby. I promise that next week I'll have more time to help you with the kids." He looked at me, then back at Marta. "Well, I think I'm going to head up to bed now. It was nice to meet you, Estrella." He leaned down and gave Marta another quick kiss. He whispered something in her ear and she smiled. Then he went to their bedroom.

Marta watched him leave. "Just because you meet the man of your dreams doesn't mean your life turns into a fairy tale."

Seeing them together made me think about Speedy. I smiled.

"And what are you smiling at, smarty pants?"

"There's this boy, from the neighborhood. I knew him when I was little, and I just re-met him again. His name is Speedy, and he's wonderful and smart and funny. And I don't know what it is, but whenever I'm around him I just feel so . . . so . . ." I looked down. "My dad has forbidden me to see him."

Marta gave me an understanding smile and we burst out laughing.

She checked her watch. "It's five-thirty. If we hurry, we can still sneak you in. Can't let you get into more trouble. I want to make sure this story ends right!"

Marta drove quickly and parked her car down the street from my house. Soft light was coming from the east as we carefully snuck around into the backyard. The sound of our feet crushing the dry grass seemed so loud in my ears.

"I can't believe I'm still sneaking around at my age," Marta joked in a hushed voice. The sun was starting to come up and Bill Clinton, Don Ramon's rooster, let out a happy morning squawk.

Marta leaned over and shushed him. "*Todavía no.* It's not morning just yet."

My bedroom window was still cracked open. Marta bent down and gave me a boost. "Thanks, Marta," I whispered down to her. "For, y'know, everything."

"No prob, little cuz," she said. "I've been there. You'll be all right."

With my free hand I raised the window and pulled myself up.

la raza (lah ʾrah-za) n., Spanish, informal: 1. It literally means the people. 2. It's also used to refer to Latino people. I've seen it used a lot on T-shirts and on the radio in reference to people from the East Side or other Spanish-speaking communities. Lots of neighborhood organizations have la raza in their name, like the La Raza Information Center and La Clinica de La Raza.

ESTRELLA!" MY MOM CALLED OUT and opened the door without knocking. "*Mija*, get up. We have practice."

I rolled over and pulled the covers over my head. "Mom, I don't feel well." The damn birds chirping outside wouldn't give me a moment's rest.

Quickly, she yanked off my fuzzy unicorn blanket and began to examine me. I was hoping that there were huge circles under my eyes. Then she gave me a worried look and felt my head for a temperature.

"*Qué te pasa?*" she asked.

I shook my head because I had no energy to reply. There was a moment of silence and she left the room. I thought I heard her say she'd cancel rehearsal. *Yes!*

I sighed in relief and tried to fall back asleep. Just as I started to drift off, a scuffing noise came from the other side of the door.

"Let me go," Nana shouted.

"Leave her alone," my mother said forcefully.

What was going on out there? It sounded like a fight. I hoped that my mother would win.

The door crashed open. Nana hurried to my bed. She must have been excited, because her usually ailing body seemed to be pretty agile at the moment.

"I came just in time," Nana huffed and straightened her black dress.

My mother stood by the door, her body rigid in refusal. "I told you, she just needs to rest."

"I will be the judge of that!" Nana retorted. "Remember, I'm the one who had eleven kids."

The look on my mother's face resembled that of a powerless child. I wondered if we both suffered from bossy-mom syndrome.

"Now go like *dis*," Nana commanded while sticking out her tongue. She began to check me out, like a doctor. She even sniffed me once or twice, which was really gross. My nana lived in a world where spirits and witches walked among us. When I was a kid, she'd told the best bedtime stories. Even though Nana was a devout Catholic, like most Mexicans, she also believed in the power of magic and spells.

"Grandma," I said in a weak voice, "I had this strange dream last night. This evil old lady was chasing me. She was throwing eyeballs at my head."

"*Hijole!*" She slapped her thigh.

"Could it be a sign?" I asked.

"*Mal de ojo?*" Nana wondered out loud.

"I give up!" my mother cried. She threw her hands up and went to leave the room.

"It's a good thing I know a little bit about healing. I'll have those evil spirits running scared." Nana winked with her good eye. She went to close my door. I sighed in relief. With Nana on my side, I knew that I could get my parents to leave me alone. But as soon as the door closed behind my mother, Nana's sweet-concerned-grandma demeanor fell away. She turned into an army sergeant and yelled, "Now get out of bed and get dressed!"

"What?"

She marched over to me and pinched my arm—hard. "*No me oyes?* Do you want me to lend you my hearing aid? Get up now!"

"But what's wrong?" I asked.

She brought her face really close to mine. I could smell her BenGay as she said, "Don't try to con me, darling. The only thing you're suffering from is from too much partying. Now, if you don't want your mommy to find out, you'll get up right now."

Damn! I got up and grabbed some shorts and a T-shirt that were lying on the floor.

"Very good. Now, you won't mind helping me to do some chores around my house."

"Of course not, Nana," I mumbled.

"Good, because my lawn is ten feet high." She raised her hand over her four-foot-nine frame. "You gonna need a machete to cut it down." I cringed at the sound of my nana's cackle.

I pulled my hair back into a ponytail and gazed into my mirror. I saw the dress Christie had given me crumpled into a ball. I remembered putting it on the night before, so excited about what the night might bring. That felt like years ago.

"Where are you two going?" my mother asked, when she saw me and Nana walking out the door. Mom was wearing her favorite Coke-bottle sunglasses and a straw sun hat. She was pruning the white azaleas in her garden patch by the driveway. It was a fresh, clear, and super-bright morning.

"There's an exorcism at twelve. If we go now, we may just be able to catch it," Nana said as she yanked me by the crook of my arm.

My mother gave us both a reluctant smile. "Have fun." She waved her white gardening gloves.

Nana's house stood out like a sore thumb with its year-round Christmas lights hanging from the roof, overgrown weed lawn, and broken windows patched with duct tape. Nana had miniature lion statues adorning her brick fence and a life-size black Labrador doll on her front porch (to scare off the undesirables).

Nana was unrelentingly strict and commanding, shouting orders and chastising me every ten minutes. After I mowed her lawn in record-breaking heat, I had to weed the forest she called a garden, then cut and peel *nopales* for her to give away to her neighbors. The only bright side was that Nana lived on the same block as Speedy. If I'd learned one thing the night before, it was how rare true friendship really was

"It's important to do things for other people," Nana said as we were sealing the last diced pieces of cactus into sandwich bags. We were sitting in her pistachio-green kitchen. The walls were adorned with framed prints of *The Last Supper*, old photographs of relatives long dead, and her favorite idols, like the Pope and the Rock. The smell of mold was everywhere, especially in her refrigerator. It was stocked with free food from the local charities and containers full of leftovers, because she did not believe in throwing anything away.

"Can I go now, Nana?" I asked. My arms were scratched from her sticky weeds. My fingers were sore from pricking myself with cactus needles. I was exhausted.

Nana looked me over silently, evaluating my efforts. "I guess you've done enough."

"Thanks!" I said, jumping out of my chair and giving her a big kiss on her soft, flabby cheek.

"Don't let me catch you trying to pull a fast one on me again," she warned from her seat at the wobbly kitchen table.

"I won't," I hollered, and ran out the door.

Cautiously, I made my way down the street toward Speedy's place. He lived in a hobbitlike peach-colored house on a patch of green Astroturf on the corner. There was a sign posted on an unpainted fence that said, NO SOLICITING. BEWARE OF HUNGRY

DOGS. I hated dogs. As if smelling my fear, one of them started barking wildly from inside.

As I approached the gate, I started losing my nerve. Maybe this was a stupid idea. Speedy probably didn't even live here anymore. Or worse, he might not want to see me. I wanted to turn back and forget about it. My pride was killing me, but I had to push forward. I had to apologize.

I opened the squeaking gate, and as if on cue, the barking became louder and more frantic. What was I going to do? Ever since Nana's real Labrador, Kojak, had attacked me as a kid, I'd been deathly afraid of dogs. The fear in my mind told me to go home, but I had come too far to turn back now. I knocked on the door.

Nobody answered.

I was about to go away when the door opened and a large man loomed before me.

"Yeah?" he said, eyeing me suspiciously. The man resembled Speedy, except he was twice as old and two times his size. On his dark, pockmarked face, he had a thick goatee that was pointy at the end, and intelligent gray eyes. His long black hair was tied in a neat braid down his back. From the look of his black leather vest, Harley-Davidson T-shirt, and steel-toed boots, I assumed he was a biker.

"Um . . ." I hesitated. "My name is Estrella Alvarez. I'm a friend of Speedy's. Is he home?"

The older man stared at me for a while. "He's not here," he said. I think he expected me to leave, but I just stood there staring at him. He sighed. "Come in. I'll leave Speedy a note that you dropped by."

After he disappeared into one of the rooms, I couldn't help but snoop around the house a little. My eyes wandered and instructed my feet to follow. It couldn't hurt to learn a little bit about Speedy's home life. The living room walls were painted gray, and the wooden floors were scuffed as if they had been trampled, like after a heavy metal concert. A lamp cast an eerie yellow glow on a huge picture of the dead *Tejano* singer Selena, who was pictured with a black panther on her lap. The picture dangled lopsidedly over the wide-screen TV. Torn brown curtains covered a glass sliding door to the right, keeping out the afternoon sun. A pesky hairless Chihuahua with extra-long whiskers jumped on me immediately, snapping at my leg as if it thought it were a ferocious pit bull. *So this is the dog the sign warned me of,* I thought.

There were numerous framed newspaper clippings of the older man who'd answered the door standing with important people like the mayor of San Jose and several California governors. Awards for community service hung alongside them. The man was a lot thinner in the pictures, so I guessed they were taken a long time ago.

I was so engrossed in poking around, I didn't hear the old man come up behind me.

"That one I took with Cesar, after a hunger strike we did together in Fresno," he said proudly.

"Cesar who?"

He looked amused. "Cesar Chavez," he said slowly, as if to remind me.

"Oh, *that* Cesar," I said. There'd been this one time Mom

wouldn't let us cross the picket line at a grocery store. "Isn't the boycott over?"

He snickered. "You're funny. Speedy told me about you."

"Are you his uncle?"

"Yeah," he said, extending his hand for me to shake. "You can call me Calaca."

"Skeleton?" I asked, unsure whether I'd heard right.

He laughed heartily. "Yeah, I got that name when I was skinny as a pencil." I liked this guy. He had a warm, comfortable way about him that reminded me of Speedy.

He looked back at the picture on the wall. "Those were crazy times. Hear this?" he said, knocking on his head. "I got a silver plate inserted after a tear gas canister cracked my skull open at a peaceful protest. Those cops were no joke. They fired on women and children like it was target practice. Cesar insisted on keeping the movement nonviolent. We were just people trying to get some dignity." He stopped, smiled at me for a second, and then started again. "Most schools won't teach you this stuff. They won't tell you how the restaurants used to have signs that read, No Dogs or Mexicans Allowed. People want to pretend that it never happened, that racism is a thing of the past. A lot of people fought hard for integration. They fought hard so that *la raza* could even go to white private schools."

"I go to a private school," I said.

He grinned. "Well, there you go. Wasn't too long ago that they had segregated schools all over California. It wasn't just the blacks; they segregated the Mexicans and the Filipinos, too."

"I see why Speedy is always bragging about you."

Calaca smiled with pride. "Speedy is a good boy, but I can't help but worry. He's my only nephew and I don't want to lose him to the streets. You know what?" His face lit up. "Speedy's out volunteering at a senior center."

Volunteering? For some reason that sounded so much like Speedy. That stuff he'd been saying about loving his community—it wasn't just talk. He was out there trying to make it a better place. "Do you know the name of the place?"

Calaca took a moment to think real hard. "The place has this crazy name. Ahh, I can't think of it. I'll let him know you stopped by."

I thanked him, but as I walked back down to the street I heard Calaca calling behind me, "I can see why Speedy talks about you."

AT SCHOOL, I WAS TOTALLY ALONE ONCE AGAIN. Sheila and Christie weren't talking to me or even looking in my direction. They walked right past me in the hall Monday morning and pretended like I wasn't there. I didn't like it, but I knew there wasn't anything I could do. The fight had happened and it was real and it mattered. We couldn't pretend like everything was the same. It was way too late to go back.

As soon as the dismissal bell rang, I went straight home.

But when I opened the door, I immediately sensed that things were not good here either, not good at all. Maybe I should have stayed away. My mom was staring at me, looking as if she were about to hit me with a thousand *chanclas*.

"I don't know what's wrong with you," my mother gasped as she paced the living room floor. I swallowed hard. *Crap!* I had forgotten that we had a meeting with the caterer and I'd been supposed to leave school early. Now I was in serious trouble. I walked to the couch with my head down and sat next to my father while my mom ranted on and on.

"How could you be so irresponsible!" she screamed. "Don't you ever think?" I sat there, gritting my teeth. I was the "good" daughter, so I was expected to keep my mouth shut and suck it up.

"You made me look like an idiot when they declined all our credit cards! Why didn't you at least warn me?" she cried.

"Mom," I tried to interject, "I'm sorry." But my words were drowned out by her voice. "I just forgot that . . ."

It took me a second to realize that my mother wasn't yelling at me. My dad had been watching an A's game. He was staring blankly at the muted screen.

"Nobody appreciates me in this family," she said. My dad rolled his eyes and grunted. He'd heard this speech a hundred times.

My dad got up and faced her. "Reyna, I'm glad they wouldn't accept your credit. Maybe now you can think sensibly about this whole thing."

Not this again, I thought. Mom was not in a sensible mood right now.

"What?" she shrieked.

"You never listen when I try to talk to you." He shook his head. "I tried to warn you. I even told you to get *padrinos* to help us out. But oh no, Reyna Alvarez is too good to ask for help, isn't she?"

"All I'm guilty of is loving my daughter enough to throw her a spectacular *quince*," she whimpered.

It was always hard to argue with my mother when she claimed that whatever crazy thing she was doing was out of love for you.

"Oh, come on, Reyna," my dad said. "You need to assume responsibility for this mess. This *quinceañera* has consumed you and our checking account. You've maxed out all our credit cards. Five hundred for an ice sculpture, seven hundred for a limo, and one thousand for a mariachi band that'll only play for twenty minutes. This is ridiculous. Estrella said she wanted a small party. But no—you want to show up every mother in the barrio!"

"I don't care what Estrella said about her party!" my mother shouted back. "I know what kind of party she needs!"

"She certainly doesn't need five hundred dollars' worth of frozen water!"

"Well, she doesn't need a cheap bastard for a father, either!"

Suddenly, I had the same feeling that I'd had at Christie's party, like something inside me was boiling. So I grabbed the first thing I could lay my hands on and threw it down on the ground. It was a lamp.

"Shut up! Shut up! Shut up!" I screamed. The crash of the lamp startled my parents. Finally, and maybe for the first time in my entire life, I had their undivided attention. "Why can't you stop fighting and listen for a second? Instead of screaming to each other about what is *best for me,* why don't you just ask me and stop all this insane yelling! I hate it and I hate you both right now!"

My mother's palm shot up and smacked me across the face.

"Don't you ever," she said, breathing heavily, "talk to us like that. Have you no respect?" My father stood beside her in frustration.

But instead of breaking down, I was fueled by her reaction. I didn't want to displease or disappoint them, but enough was enough. "God damn it!" I screamed making a fist in the air. "Don't I have a right to live my own life? *You* have no respect for *me,* and I won't take it anymore!" I knew I'd crossed some line, but I didn't care. "Mom, you never hear me when I tell you what I want! You think you know better than I do about what's going to make me happy, but you're wrong. *I* know what's best for me."

Tears were rolling down my cheeks at this point. I stepped in front of my father and stood toe-to-toe with him. "Dad, I'm almost a grown woman, but you guys keep treating me like a child. If you don't let me start making my own decisions now, I'm never going to know how to do it!"

And then I stood in front of both of them. "Don't I ever get to be happy? You never ask me what I want. All you care about is yourselves! You two are fighting over a stupid *quince* that I never wanted in the first place. I'm not you, Mom. Don't you get that?" The tears kept coming. "I'll never be like you." I looked up with blurry eyes and saw a pained look on my mother's face.

She didn't say a word, but I could tell she was about to cry.

Her eyes took me in without seeing me. I wondered what she was thinking. She fumbled for the broken pieces of cracked ceramic that littered the ground. It was her favorite lamp.

"Fine," she said while wiping at her eyes. "You think you're so grown up. Do whatever you want then." Her voice sounded far away and hollow, as if she were talking through a long tube. "You don't want a stupid *quinceañera*. Then we won't have one. We'll cancel it." Her shoulders hunched over in defeat, she went into her room, where her wailing got louder.

My dad stood there, helpless. "Reyna," he called out, but my mother ignored him.

I was too startled to say anything.

Dad turned to me. He looked like he'd just worked a hundred overtime hours with no rest. "*What's the matter with you?*" he said sternly. "You have no heart." I knew he wanted to say more, but he just stomped out the room.

"Dad, I'm sorry."

He stopped at the door. I wanted him to tell me that he loved me. That Mom would get over it and life would go back to normal, but he didn't. He just shook his head sadly. Then he walked out the back door to sit in his Impala.

Mom was crushed and cried for most of the evening. She was too upset to cook. I thought about trying to make something simple, maybe some quesadillas, but Rey ordered a pizza before I had a chance. An uncomfortable silence lingered around us as we sat down to eat. Dad was extremely moody and barked at me and my brothers as if he were ready to beat someone up. Bobby and Rey gave me heated glances as they ate. It was obvious they thought I was to blame for the whole mess. Then the phone rang.

"Mom," Bobby said, holding the phone and chewing at the same time, "it's the mariachi group. They said your check bounced."

My dad's hand came down and crashed into the table with a loud thump. "Not again!" he said angrily. My mother just sat there staring at the cold slice of pizza she hadn't touched. Then she put her head in her hands and started sobbing.

My dad mumbled something that none of us could really hear and stormed out the back door. The moment the door slammed, my mother ran crying to her bedroom.

Bobby and Rey both gave me disapproving nods and went to shoot monsters on their PlayStation.

As for me, I went to my room, too. I picked up a scrapbook that my mom had made me when I was a kid. Turning the pages, I remembered how happy we used to all be. There was a picture of my mom and dad in their twenties. Even with the funny hair-dos and weird clothes, I could see how in love they were. There was a photo of my brothers and Nana on Halloween when they'd dressed up like WWE wrestlers. And then there was one of my christening. My mom was holding me in her arms. I was gazing up at her and she was looking down at me adoringly.

Then I read what my mom had written underneath that picture.

Mi hija, la luz de mi vida. My daughter, the light of my life.

ESTRELLÍTA!" TÍA LUCKY YELLED OUT from the living room. "Where are you?"

I was preparing to study for a math quiz, piling up my homework notebooks. It was strange hearing someone call my name in my house. Or at all. It was two days later and no one was really speaking to me. No one at school and no one at home. I walked out into the hallway to see what *Tía* wanted. Most likely, she was going to tell me how I'd ruined her life, too.

Tía Lucky was wearing a brown sequined top (two sizes too small), black stretch pants, and spike heels. She looked like she was going out on the town, even though she was just hanging around my house. *Tía* was holding a big white bag in her left hand.

"It's done!" she exclaimed.

"What are you talking about?" I groaned before plopping myself down on the couch. The house felt cold and empty. Everything had changed in the past couple of days. Mom had stopped filling the kitchen with the sweet smells of food and her really bad singing that used to always embarrass me. I kind of missed it. My dad wasn't cracking any jokes anymore either. And my brothers had only been home to sleep. It felt like some aliens had captured my family and replaced them with dull strangers. I wanted my family back.

Tía Lucky pressed the garment bag to her chest. "The dress, *mensa*. It took a while, I know—"

"*Tía*, the *quince* is canceled." Hadn't she heard?

She ignored me, as always, and shoved the dress in my face. "Try it on. I'm sure it'll look lovely on you."

"*Tía*," I moaned. This was stupid! What was the point of trying on the dress?

"Just put it on." She gave it to me with a big smile, as if she had the winning Lotto ticket in her hands.

I knew I couldn't dissuade her. She was *terca*. I grabbed the dress and went into the bathroom.

"Come out when you're done," she shouted as I closed the door.

I peeled off my clothes and looked at the tangerine-swirl material in the bag. An image of Marta in her dress flashed before me. I couldn't help but laugh as I thought about what she'd have said about all this. I wondered if I'd topped Marta by being an even bigger bitch. I lifted the dress out of the bag and felt a lump in my chest. My mother had been so excited about this, and now here I was—the dress was finally ready, but she hated me. Both of my parents did. I wondered if they'd disown me now, like *Tía* Lucky had Marta. I tried to imagine myself without my family. I thought about Speedy and what he'd said about appreciating his mom now that his father was dead. And then I missed Speedy, too. All of this was going through my head as I pulled the soft satin over my head. It felt snug and warm on my skin.

"Hurry up," my *tía* said impatiently.

"Just a minute," I snapped. *Well, I guess it couldn't hurt to show my* tía *what could have been*, I thought as I opened the door slowly.

When I came into view, *Tía* Lucky reacted like she'd been slapped on the butt. *This dress must look horrible!* I thought. I was glad it was only my *tía* who was there to see me. A tear fell down Lucky's face and dripped off her chin.

"Estrellíta," she whispered, "you look so beautiful." Then her face opened up into a huge smile. "Let me zip you up in the back." She turned me around and pulled gently on the zipper. "Just wait until you see this, *mija*, you are not going to believe. . . ." She dragged me into my mother's bedroom and stood me in front of the full-length mirror.

"*Mija*," she said, "look."

The dress had been completely transformed—it was no longer the ugly thing Marta had worn. Instead, it was this glamorous gown. The cascading fabric fell down in rippling waves. I couldn't believe how the orange color actually flattered my skin tone, giving me a warm, soft, honey-colored glow. The dress hugged my curves. It wrapped tightly around the waist and hung loosely over my hips.

"Oh my God," I said slowly. "I'm gorgeous!"

"Yes, you are," *Tía* agreed.

"*Tía!*" I cried. "It's so beautiful." I twirled around in place, marveling as the material swirled around me.

Lucky smiled and gazed at me with a misty look in her eyes. "We've dreamed of this moment ever since you were born."

By "we," she meant my mother and her.

"It's what we always wanted as little girls." She sat down on the bed and patted the space next to her. I sat down because I knew we were on the verge of a confession.

"Growing up, there was never any money," my *tía* began. "Your nana worked cleaning office buildings at night and in a restaurant during the day. Your *mamá* was the oldest and had to take care of all us kids. We used to have to share a bed, all four of us girls. It was like weenies in a wrapper." She giggled and scrunched up her shoulders to show me how tight they slept. "Your *mamá* and I would whisper to each other late into the night. We dreamed of having our own *quinceañeras*. And we would bicker over hairstyles and dresses. In those times, only the rich girls had them. Your mom and I always felt inferior to the rich Mexican girls at school." Her face became hard, then pained, as if the memory were draining her of blood.

I took her hand and squeezed it. My *tía* was always cool and collected. I wasn't used to seeing her like this.

She continued. "We didn't want you girls to ever feel that you were less than anyone else." She sniffed loudly as her fat tears wet my outstretched hand. "I wanted my daughter to have the best *quinceañera.*" Her voice sounded strained. "Even though she was a little chunky, I wanted her to know that she was beautiful inside." She paused as if remembering something. "Maybe I was a little too hard on her. You always wish you could've done things better upon hindsight."

The dreamy look in her eyes told me that she missed her daughter. My *tía's* pride kept her from admitting it. I considered telling her about my visit with Marta. Her grandchildren were getting so big. But I held back. Marta and *Tía's bronca* felt like a whole new tangled mess. I had enough trouble in my life without bringing my *tía* into the mix.

"*Tía*, I really screwed things up, didn't I?" I said. I stood up and felt the material swirl around me. I ran my hands over the skirt. The fabric felt so smooth, like silk.

She reached out and touched my face. "Inpatient, that's what you are. I don't know why you kids are in such a hurry to grow up." She laughed. "But that's what makes you a teenager."

"My mom hates me."

"No, she doesn't," my *tía* said. "She loves you more than her own life."

"But I ruined all her dreams." I looked around the room. *Quinceañera* catalogs were still stacked up on my mother's small wooden night table, next to her reading glasses. My tiara rested on her dresser next to a small ceramic vase of fake flowers.

I sat back down on the bed and my *tía* wrapped her arms

around me. Then she started to rock me back and forth as if I were a child. I felt warm and comforted and finally understood. The last time I'd felt like that, I'd been with Marta.

"I think your mother made the same mistake that I did with Marta."

I looked up into her eyes. "How so?"

"We got lost and forced our dreams upon you. We forgot the most important thing about the *quinceañera*. It's *your* day."

"So you don't think I ruined the family?"

My *tía* burst out laughing. "Don't be *loca*."

"But Dad and Mom hate each other."

"Those two would bicker about the color of the sky. You can't think that it has anything to do with you."

"But I don't like seeing them like that."

"Well . . ." My *tía* paused. "You took care of that, didn't you? Now they have no *quinceañera* to fight about."

I cringed, remembering the horrible things I'd said to my parents. Would they ever forgive me?

I grabbed my *tía* urgently. "Please help me! I have to bring this family back together."

"That's no small order, *chiquita*." My *tía* shook her head as if it were hopeless. "From what Reyna told me, the family's broke. Looks like you guys will be eating rice and beans for months. There's always the lottery, but I hear that you have a better chance of getting hit by a bus."

The oval mirror in front of us reflected our images. I couldn't help but admire myself in the *quince* dress. As kids, Tere, Izzy, and I had played *quinceañera*. We'd put on Tere's older sister's dresses and smear our faces with makeup and put jewelry in our hair. I remembered one time Izzy and I had gotten into a punching match because we couldn't decide who would have more bows on her dress. But aside from all the ceremonial and partying stuff, the *quinceañera* had been important to us because it would mean that we were all grown up. I looked at my reflection and wondered, Estrella, are you ready to grow up?

I felt a sudden surge, like something inside me was shifting. "*Tía*," I said, "it can't be impossible."

"I didn't say it was impossible," she stated. "It'll just be tricky." My *tía* squeezed my hand. I realized that I'd misjudged her. Underneath the shallow, tacky, cover girl exterior, there was a strong and wise woman. I was proud that she was my *tía*.

"*Mija*, you shouldn't do anything just to make your mother happy," she said.

"No, I won't. Well, I am, but I'm not."

Tía looked very confused. "What do you mean?"

It was hard to explain, so I dug deep for the right words.

"I need to bring everyone together and show them how much they mean to me. And I need to show myself that I can be me—the *real* me."

Tía pulled me into another tight hug. "That's the best thing I've ever heard."

"I'm going to go change out of this beautiful dress so we can hide it before my parents get back. Thank you, *Tía*!"

And for the first time in a long while, I knew exactly what I needed to do next.

★ 23 ★

> **perdón** (pear-'dohn) v., Spanish, formal: 1. to forgive or ask for forgiveness 2. It's like saying sorry, but in a more formal way. Like if you do something really, really bad. Or you do something that offends your elders. 3. most commonly used with old people

I TOOK A DEEP BREATH, smoothed my hair back, and pulled up my collar. Then I knocked on the door.

Izzy rolled her eyes the minute she saw me.

"What the hell do you want?" she shouted over the deafening sounds of Molotov.

"I want to talk to you," I shouted back.

Izzy huffed and slammed the door in my face.

I banged on the door again, but Izzy turned up the music to drown out all the noise I was making.

I went around the house and tried to use the back door, but it was locked. However, the window to her mom's bedroom was cracked open. I stepped on the recycling bin to reach the window and then I pushed it up and climbed through, falling over a small desk covered with perfume bottles and framed photographs.

Her mother's room looked exactly the same as it had when I was a little girl. Everything was so frilly and feminine, so unlike Izzy.

I went into the living room, which was lit only by the glow of the TV screen. Izzy was sprawled out on the couch, trying on red lipstick in a small mirror, bobbing her head to the music.

"Izzy," I yelled, "can we talk?"

She looked up at me, surprised, and quickly wiped the lipstick off with the back of her hand.

"What the hell are you doing in here?" Izzy said. The room smelled like microwaved burritos.

"I'm sorry about breaking in, but I have to talk to you."

"Damn, Estrella! Don't you know when to quit?" She marched over to the front door. "Get out of my house!"

"I will not leave until you listen to me," I said defiantly and planted myself on her black recliner.

Izzy huffed and grabbed two remotes like a gunslinger. She pointed one and down went the stereo. She aimed the other at the TV and *zap*—off it went.

"You have one minute," Izzy fumed. "Then I want you out of here and out of my life forever." She placed her hands on her hips and waited for me to continue.

"I came to apologize."

"Aghh!" Izzy groaned, collapsing into the couch opposite me. "Estrella, don't you get it? I'm tired of your apologies. They mean nothing to me. You're a two-faced, spoiled brat. Why don't you just run off with your little rich private-school friends?"

"I am not spoiled," I said.

"Yes, you are! You're so spoiled, you don't even realize it!"

"You don't even know what you're talking about. Try living with two parents who never listen to a word you say." I stood up and squared off against her.

"You should be thankful your parents love you enough to throw you a *quinceañera*. You make me so sick!" Izzy got up and shoved me on the shoulder. "You're complaining about having a big party with expensive dresses, a limo. And all you can do is shit on it. You need to go!"

The shock on my face was apparent.

"Yeah, I heard," Izzy said, pushing me again. "Your mom called my mom all in tears the other day. Don't you have any feelings?"

"Stop pushing me," I snapped and pushed her back.

Izzy grabbed my hair and tried to toss me to the ground. I held on tight to her black shirt. We both fell, tumbling to the floor. We squirmed, fingers scratching and arms locking around each other.

"God damn it, Estrella," Izzy huffed. With her free hand, she jabbed my ribs. I grabbed her hands and pinned both her arms down, but then she head-butted me—and that girl has a thick head. I howled.

Quickly, we moved apart to opposite sides of the living room floor. My skull was throbbing. If I'd been in a cartoon, little tweeting birds would have been flying around my head. There was no sound except for our heavy breathing.

"That hurt," I squealed.

Izzy wiped sweat from her brow. "That's for ditching us."

"I said I was sorry."

"Sometimes saying sorry isn't good enough." Izzy grimaced as she rubbed her ribs. Her face was flushed and there was a small scratch right above her eye.

"I want you to forgive me," I said through clenched teeth.

"That's why you started a fight?"

"I didn't start it. You did!"

"You think that by beating people up you'll force them to like you?"

"You're ridiculous!" I said. "Yes! Okay, I messed up. I realize that now. And I've been feeling horrible ever since I saw you at Tere's *quince*. If you'd let me talk, you'd know that."

Izzy was speechless, for once.

"You were right all along. Yes, I did ditch you and Tere when I went to Sacred Heart. I thought that my new friends would be better, that I would be better. But I'm not. I'm the same old Alvarez who used to kick your ass."

I saw a small smile creep across Izzy's face.

"I'm not proud of how I treated you guys. But you once told me that we were homegirls. Homegirls are sisters, so here." I passed her the small package I had tucked in my back pocket.

"What's this?" she asked, holding the white box. She started to open it but reconsidered and said, "Don't think you can bribe me like your snotty friends."

"It's not a bribe, Izzy!" I said. Then I softened my voice. "It's just something I should have done a long time ago."

Izzy unwrapped the gift and pulled out a gold necklace with a plate that said *Homegirls* in cursive.

"I got one for Tere, too," I said softly.

"This doesn't change anything," Izzy muttered. She dropped the necklace back into the paper.

"C'mon, Izzy." I pulled down my collar. "See, I got one too. It's to remind us that no matter where we go, we'll always be homegirls. Isn't that what you told me?"

"What do you care about what I say? You proved to me and Tere that we aren't important enough to be your homegirls."

"That's not true."

"Did your white friends dump you?"

"What?"

Izzy sneered at me. "I figure the people you thought were your friends turned on you and now you're coming back to us."

"That's not what happened."

"So then why don't you give this to them? We haven't been homegirls for a long time."

"Fine," I said in frustration. "You're right. I wanted them to be my homegirls. But I realized that they weren't really my friends, just like you said. Real friends accept you as you are. They don't try to change you."

Izzy was staring at me as if she'd just witnessed hell freezing over. I kind of enjoyed the shocked look on her face. Slowly, Izzy picked up the chain and twirled the gold plate in her hand. She said nothing.

"That's it," I said, getting up to go.

There was a pause before Izzy asked, "And you got one for Tere, too?" She still wasn't looking directly at me.

"How could I leave out Tere?"

Izzy laughed. "She wouldn't let you, even if you tried." She unhooked the necklace and tried to put it around her neck. Then she stopped and looked up. "The least you can do is help me with this, after that beatin' you gave me."

I helped her fasten the necklace and smiled. It was a hell of a lot better to be Izzy's friend than her enemy.

"Come on." Izzy grabbed my hand and gave me a smirk. "Let's go find Tere. Maybe you can beat her up, too!"

> **padrino** (pah-'dree-noh) n., Spanish, formal: 1. god-father 2. When used in a wedding or quince cere-mony, it is the honorable title for a person who assists in the celebration. 3. People use padrinos and madrinas to cut costs. For example, you can have a madrina who pays for the band and another who pays for the band's food.

T HE NEXT EVENING, IZZY AND I MET at Tere's house to go over plans for my *quinceañera*. We'd spent most of the previous night together, talking and trying to understand where we'd all gone wrong with each other over the past few years. Finally they'd agreed that a good way for us all to rebuild our friendship was to help me fix all the damage I'd done.

"Estrella!" Izzy and Tere shouted pulling me out of my day-dream. "Did you do it yet or not?"

"Huh?" I asked.

"Book the church! *Qué te pasa?*"

Tere's bedroom felt small with all its bulky wood furniture and because she shared it with her two older sisters. She had a corner next to her bed to call her own, where she kept her hair products, pencils, and makeup scattered all over a desk. Izzy was holding Tere's *quince* photo album in her hand, and she looked like she was ready to throw it at me.

I smiled, feeling embarrassed. My mind had a will of its own and crept over to Speedy at the most inopportune moments. I missed him so much, and I'd almost dialed his number two dozen times. But I always got too scared and hung up at the last second. At least with the *quince*, everything was turning out better than I'd imagined. Tere and Izzy were more than eager to help me organize the party, and my brothers were willing to do anything to get Mom and Dad back together. My *tía* was helpful—sometimes a bit too helpful—but she did consult me before making any major decisions. Best of all, Amy (from Juana's boutique) had agreed to donate a bunch of decorations that her mother had been going to throw away. So far we hadn't spent a cent, which wasn't saying much, because we still didn't have mariachis, food, transportation, or a cake.

"Sorry, my mind slipped."

"You were thinking about Speedy again, weren't you?" Izzy teased.

"No, I wasn't!"

"You lie!" Izzy snapped. "I can tell when you're lying, 'cause you're not very good at it."

"Okay, so maybe I *was* thinking about him. But it's pointless."

"Why?" Tere asked.

"Because he hates her," Izzy said. Then she filled Tere in on the details.

"You should stop by his house again," Tere said. "Guys like it when a girl is assertive."

"He's not like most guys. Besides, like I said, it's hopeless. He'll never want to speak to me again. Can we talk about something else now? Like the *quince*?"

"Touchy, aren't we?" Tere smirked. She redid her ponytail in a restless manner. Her cat's-eye reading glasses and the clipboard in her hand made her look very professional. She was taking her role as *quince* assistant very seriously.

Izzy unlaced her combat boots to get more comfortable. "C'mon, Tere. I'd like to get this over with before my butt falls asleep."

"Yeah," I chimed in. It felt like we'd been going over *quince* plans for hours. I'd been adamant with my *tía* and Tere—I wasn't going to take any loans or go into debt for this party. There had to be a better way.

Tere reviewed her very short list. "So we got the church date all set?"

"Check. My *tía* and I went over there yesterday to talk to the priest."

"Decorations?"

"Check." Izzy saluted as if she were an army cadet. "I just got off the phone with Amy, and she said that if we can pitch in for the materials, she will also do the dove *recuerdos*."

"Reception?"

"The house," I said. Tere shook her head in disapproval. "It's the only place I can think of that won't charge us my firstborn. Besides, my brothers are going to clean it all up and make it look real nice."

This didn't convince Tere. "Estrella, this isn't just some backyard barbecue. This is your *quinceañera*. It's a once-in-a-lifetime event."

"I know, but my *tía* is getting these tents from her friend that'll totally transform the space."

Tere looked at me skeptically.

"Trust me," I pleaded.

"We still haven't talked about the music."

"Oh, Marta said Suave can DJ," I said.

"No," Tere cut in, "I mean the mariachis."

"Can't," Izzy said while pulling out a list from her back jeans pocket. "I called all over town, and no one is willing to do it for under a hundred bucks."

"Hey, why aren't we using *padrinos*?" Tere asked.

"Are you serious?" Not the *padrinos* plan again. It was true that *padrinos* would alleviate a lot of my stress and spread costs around. However, a part of me felt very uncomfortable asking people for financial help. Maybe it ran in my genes—my mother hadn't wanted to have *padrinos* either.

"That's how we did mine. How do you think we paid for everything? There must have been like a hundred *padrinos*. It's a big deal. Everyone wants to be a *padrino*."

"You're totally exaggerating," Izzy mumbled as she stuffed her mouth with Hot Cheetos.

"Well, maybe a little." Tere gave Izzy a cheeky smile. "But what matters is, that's how we did it. We put each person in charge of something and then put their names on the invitation. I'm sure it saved my mom a ton of dough and headaches."

"But who can I ask?" I said.

"You act so *mensa* sometimes, Estrella," Tere kidded. "Your parents know hella people. And you have nothing to lose. The worst they could do is say no."

Tere was right. There was nothing to lose. I reached into my book bag and pulled out my binder where I kept all my *quince* stuff. "Here's my mom's guest list. Oh my God! There are so many people." I started reading from the top. "The Riveras, the Ortizes, the Ruizes, the Dominguezes."

"Dominguez, that's perfect. Now, we have someone to bring the cake." Izzy laughed. Pedro and Maria Dominguez owned the local bakery.

"What's this?" Tere asked, taking my binder out of my hand. It had a clear slipcover that I'd jammed with cheesy photographs of Sheila, Christie, and me clowning around in the mall photo booth. In one picture, Sheila was pretending to pick her nose. In another, we were all sticking our tongues out. There was a funny one where we were acting like zombies, about to eat each other's heads. And then there was the picture where we were laughing hysterically because I'd just made a joke right before the camera went off.

Tere giggled at the poses. "Are these your school friends?"

I felt a little awkward. Even though I was friends with Tere and Izzy again, I still missed Christie and Sheila. They would have enjoyed organizing this party. *But would they want to do it on a zero budget?*

"That's Christie and that's Sheila," I said, pointing them out in the photos.

"They look nice," Tere smiled.

"Yeah. They were good friends. And really fun to be around."

"Are they coming to the *quinceañera*?" Izzy asked.

"I don't think so." I scrunched my nose and shook my head. "We kind of had this huge fight." I flopped down onto Tere's twin bed.

"You smacked them, didn't you?" Izzy said, laughing uncontrollably on the floor.

"No," I smiled. "But a good catfight might have been better than what actually happened."

Izzy and Tere stared at me and waited for the whole story.

"Well, you don't know what it's like at my school. There's all kinds of pressure to have lots of money and be rich or whatever. Sheila and Christie kind of took me under their wings. They gave me all these nice clothes and brought me to these super-tight places. Then they tried to set me up with this guy Kevin, and he turned out to be this big jerk and I got mad and . . . I don't know. After that, things just sort of spun out of control. I guess I'd kind of gotten caught up in their world and tried to be like them. And then they got caught up in trying to make me over. In the end, I was acting like this whole other person, and it was just really messed up."

Izzy shook her head in disapproval.

"The worst was when I realized that they didn't really know

me at all. They knew this other person, this girl who I was pretending to be when I was around them. But whatever. I don't really care anymore," I lied.

"Well, if those girls were really your friends," Tere said, "they would want to come to your *quinceañera*. That's what friends do for each other."

"Well, that'll never happen," I said, remembering Sheila and Christie's faces when I'd left the party. I wanted to change the subject. "Let's go over that guest list."

Tere grabbed the list from my hands. She skimmed through the names. "Okay, let's try and contact the people that you know first."

"You mean, just go up to them and say, 'Hey, will you give me money for my party?'" I squirmed at the thought. Asking people for favors made me feel weak and needy—I was nobody's charity case.

"It wouldn't look right if we did it for you," Izzy said. "You have to do it."

"Fine," I said harshly. This must be that part of growing up that nobody warned you about. The part when you have to stand on your own. I just hoped I had the balance to do it.

The next evening Tere, Izzy, and I piled into Marta's car. Her kids were at the park with Mario. The inside of the car was littered with animal-cracker heads and random toys. It was early, but already the traffic was congested. Nobody liked to use public transportation. The buses took hella long and didn't come by that often. Marta parked the car in front of a corner restaurant.

"You can do it, Estrella," Tere said with a big cheesy smile.

She and Izzy had come along for encouragement. They'd wanted to come inside with me, but I'd told them that this was something I had to do alone.

"*Sí, se puede!*" Izzy and Marta chanted as I got out of the car, laughing. I was glad they had come along.

When I walked into the festive atmosphere of Taquería 2000, my stomach started to do flip-flops. Bright colorful serapes and huge pieces of Mexican pottery decorated the walls, along with murals of guitar-slinging cowboys and smiling *señoritas*. Margarita was in the kitchen, making tortillas by hand. The sound of diners clapping echoed along with the sweating accordion player, who was in the corner singing his heart out.

"Hi, Margarita," I said, shyly stepping into her feverish kitchen. The cooks and waitstaff were hollering orders back and forth. The commotion of pots and pans crashing to the ground and people shouting angrily really made me nervous.

"Hey, *mija*." Margarita smiled. She offered me her plump cheek to kiss. Her hands were moving expertly fast, patting the rolled pieces of dough into flat, round tortillas.

"I'm sorry, Margarita. Is this a bad time?"

She peered over the counter without slowing down a bit. "Are you here with your folks?"

"No, I'm by myself. I came to ask you a favor."

"*A ver?*" she asked.

I took a deep breath. "I'm having a *quinceañera*, and I would be grateful if you would be my *madrina*," I blurted out.

Her hands stopped. She wiped them on her spotted apron and gave me a big heartfelt hug. "*Ay, mija,*" she said. "I would love to be your *madrina*. I'm so proud of you and that big scholarship you won."

"You know about the scholarship?" I asked in surprise.

"Of course I do. Your parents are so proud, they won't stop talking about it. I would love to help. Let me cater the reception."

"I can't let you do all that!" I said, shocked. "I mean, that's a lot to do." I'd just been planning on asking her to bring one or two dishes and maybe some tortillas.

"*Mija*, I've known you since before you can even remember. I might not be related to you by blood, but still you are part of my community and therefore a part of my *familia*. I, along with everyone else in *el barrio*, have watched you grow up. And I like to think that in some small way, just by being here, I've been a part of that. So it would be an honor for me to contribute to your *quinceañera* in whatever way I can. Let me do this."

"Thank you, Margarita." We hugged.

As I walked out the door, I had a warm feeling in the pit of my stomach. A few of Margarita's words echoed in my mind.

Your parents are so proud of you.

I pulled out my cell phone and took the guest list out of my pocket.

I was no longer nervous about what I was about to do. Something was growing inside of me, a feeling I hadn't had in a long time—I was part of something bigger. I truly belonged. I pressed the digits on my phone.

"Hello, *Señora* Lopez? It's Estrella Alvarez. . . ."

★ 25 ★

chismosa (cheez-'moe-sah) n., Spanish, informal:
1. English translation: a gossip 2. When your neighbors are all up in your business, like they think your
life is some reality show on Fox, made for their
entertainment, they are chismosas. Or when my
nana starts telling all my innermost secrets to
strangers, like when I got my first bra. I swear, everyone at her church group knew, because they all com-
mented on how nice I was developing. Gross!

USUALLY I CAUGHT THE BUS HOME or Mom picked me up in
her grimy minivan, but I was surprised to see Nana waiting for
me on a cold, dismal day a few days later. Her pudgy cinnamon-
colored hands were snuggled into her armpits for warmth, and
she was looking down at her tan hospital shoes as if she'd forgotten if they were tied.

I tapped her on the shoulder.

Nana flinched as if she were in a trance.

"What are you doing here?" I asked. Nana looked like a peasant from the mountains in her brown lint-ridden frock and kerchief knotted under her chin.

"It's a miracle!" she exclaimed. "I prayed that you would come, and look—you're here!"

I shushed her and gently pulled her by the crook of her arm away from the front of the school, walking her a few yards until we were safely out of eavesdropping distance.

"I was so excited that I couldn't wait," Nana said. She reached into her pocket and pulled out a wad of cash. "We made a killing at the fair. It was really Agapito's idea. Such a smart boy. He's been instrumental in helping the Gray Panthers raise money for your *quinceañera*."

Nana continued rambling, but I was no longer paying attention. *Did she just say* Agapito?

"Nana," I interrupted, "are you talking about the same Agapito I knew from childhood?" I was sure there was only one Agapito. There had to be. It was such an uncommon, old-fashioned Mexican name. But then again, this was San Jose.

"Yes, the little boy who used to dance with you in the *Cinco de Mayo* parades."

"Where is he, Nana?" I said, ready to run and find him. I couldn't believe that Speedy and Nana had known each other all this time. Then everything made sense. Speedy had been out volunteering that day I'd gone to apologize, and he must have been working at my nana's senior center.

"Come on, Nana," I said, pulling her toward the bus stop. If Speedy was helping Nana to raise money, that meant that he knew all about my *quinceañera*. That didn't surprise me a bit, because Nana was a *chismosa*. She always told total strangers all our family business. But for some crazy reason, it didn't bother me one bit this time. What if Nana was right? If Speedy had done all this for my *quinceañera*, even after everything that had happened between us, that must mean something . . . but what? I had to find out, and I had to find out *now*!

We arrived at Nana's senior center parking lot just as I felt the first drops of rain fall on my head. Inside, the main room was humming with activity. Little old ladies with cotton-candy hair-dos were scrambling around, packing cakes into boxes. Speedy was standing at the center of all the business like a beacon. He was holding a clipboard and barking orders to a few meaty guys who were carrying the boxes to the back. My heart swooned at the sight of him. He looked so professional and grown-up.

My nana shuffled into the room at a determined pace "Agapito!" she shouted. "This is the granddaughter I told you about, the one you used to dance with when you were children."

"Estrella?" Speedy gasped. His hand jerked back to his hair as if he were afraid that it was sticking up and out of place.

"Speedy," I said. Our eyes met. I felt like I could barely breathe.

Nana sensed my reservation, so she pushed me forward. "Agapito made me promise not to tell you, but you know I'm no good at keeping secrets."

Thank you, Nana! I wanted to scream and cover her with kisses. "For once, you've done right." I looked up into Speedy's beautiful butterscotch-brown eyes. I'd planned this out so many times, what I wanted to say to him. But all of a sudden the words rushed out of my head.

"Speedy," I said, reaching out to him.

He jerked back. "Naw, it ain't like that," he said. "You can't come here and expect everything to be cool. You treated me like crap. Twice." He shook his head. "I don't even know why you're here."

"I'm sorry, Speedy. I really am. I was a total jerk to you. But my nana said you helped raise money for my *quinceañera* and I just thought that maybe—"

"Don't worry about it," he said flatly.

"But I . . ."

He shifted his weight nervously and stared at me without blinking much.

"Agapito!" one of the workers called out.

Speedy turned to me. "Like I said, don't worry about the money. The Panthers fundraise every month to help people in the community. These cakes here are for Local 1011, the hotel workers who're on strike. It was really your nana who nominated you. You should thank *her* for the charity."

Speedy turned to leave, but I wasn't ready to give up. He was worth fighting for. "Well, at least let me help with what you're doing now," I said. "You're raising money for striking workers, right?"

Speedy did a double take, not believing his ears. "You wanna help? I never thought I'd hear Estrella Alvarez talk about helping someone else out."

"Oh, come on. You make me sound like a self-centered brat."

He just looked at me and raised his eyebrows.

An assembly line of old ladies was bagging cakes. I started to help Nana's friend Carmen tie the boxes with string. Speedy just stood there watching me.

After the cakes were packed and loaded on a truck, we went to a busy street corner, set up a little table underneath a tent, and sold the cakes. A lot of people came out, despite the yucky weather. The money was to go to the striking workers who were fighting for better pay and health benefits. And I was glad I could help them.

By dinnertime, Nana and all her friends were ready to go home. Speedy was loading empty trays into the truck.

"Speedy, I'm not proud of the way I treated you," I said, looking down with shame. It was hard to admit that, but it was even harder to not say anything. "There's no excuse for what I did, except that I was stupid. I was trying to get away from the people who make me *me*. But that isn't right. I need my family, and I need our community," I said as I reached out my hand to him. "Most of all, I need you."

Speedy looked at my hand as if it were about to slap him.

Then my nana swatted him on the back. "Take the girl's hand," she insisted. "It's not every day Estrella admits she's been a bonehead!"

My cheeks burned and my ears started to pound. Had she been listening the entire time?

Speedy seemed to take it in stride and shook my hand.

"Very good," Nana cheered and took us both in her arms. "We better hurry. You know how your mother gets when you're late." Then Nana looked at Speedy. "Agapito, would like to join us for dinner? I'm sure it'll be okay."

"No, Nana—you can't!" I protested. My dad would really flip out.

Speedy shook his head as if he believed that I hadn't changed. I tried to explain. "See, my parents are pissed at each other right now. The *quinceañera* kind of blew up in their faces. And my dad doesn't want me to date at all. I promised him that I would concentrate on my studies."

"He's one to talk," Nana said. "He was the biggest macho in high school. Had like a hundred girlfriends. Never understood what *mi* Reyna saw in him. You leave *Señor* Alvarez to me."

I gave her a grateful smile when she took both of our hands.

"I'll come up with a plan before dinner," she added.

Speedy sat next to me on the bus. Nana was a discreet distance away, but she peered over her shoulder every now and then. I loved looking at Speedy's chiseled profile and wavy lips. He was just so damn cute. I wanted to reach out and touch the dimple in his cheek.

"So what's the deal with this senior center? When did you get involved?"

Speedy blushed. It was the first time I'd seen him really lose his cool. "Well, I had these community service hours to do at my school. You see, I kind of like to cook," he said shyly. "When the ladies found out, they made me bake sale coordinator. I recognized your nana right away. She hasn't changed a bit. When she mentioned what you were trying to do, I pushed the group to surpass our quota. I guess I was impressed that you were setting this all up. I wanted to tell you, but after our fight . . ."

I understood him completely. Actually, it felt like the first time I'd really understood anyone.

I smiled and took his hand. Then I noticed that Speedy's leg kept shaking restlessly. "Are you nervous about meeting my dad?"

"A little."

"Me too." I gave his hand a squeeze.

We got home just as my mother was setting the table. Nana walked in ahead of us. I could smell the enchiladas from outside. My stomach rumbled in anticipation of the mouthwatering dish. Speedy heard it, and my cheeks burned hot.

"You must be as hungry as me," he said.

"Dinner's ready and she's not home yet," my mother said. We were late, and Mom sounded pissed.

Bobby looked up and did a double take when he saw Speedy. Then Rey turned to see who was at the door. My dad stood up from his chair. His napkin hung from his shirt collar. Mom finally looked up and gasped when she noticed that we had company.

"*Qué es esto?*" my dad asked, flinging his napkin down on the table. He blinked as if he couldn't believe what he was seeing.

Speedy and I hesitated at the door. I stepped back, ready to flee if necessary.

Nana grabbed Speedy by the hand and pulled him inside. "I've brought a friend from my senior center."

My mother wiped her hands on her apron and greeted Speedy politely, but she didn't seem to recognize him.

"Reyna, you remember Agapito?" Nana asked with pride.

"Oh my God!" my mother said, taking him into an embrace. "*Mijo*, look at you. You're so big now."

My dad's mouth hung open.

Bobby and Rey just stared at me. They were probably thinking to themselves, *What the hell is Estrella up to?*

Mom directed Speedy to the chair next to her, forgetting all about me. "I'm sorry," she said. "We weren't expecting company. All we have is enchiladas. I hope you don't mind."

"What's this?" my dad asked again. He seemed upset that my imposing grandmother had ignored him.

"This is family dinner," Nana stated, as if she were talking to an annoyingly inquisitive child. She shook her head and mumbled under her breath while she got a chair from the kitchen. Nana had always thought Dad was a bit dense.

My mother set the table for two extra people. "I hope that there'll be enough for everyone."

"That's no problem," Nana said, getting up. "I can always cook up something—"

"No!" we all yelled. Nana had lost her sense of taste years ago at a chili cook-off in Fresno. Now she added way too much chili to everything to compensate. We didn't want to let her near anything in the kitchen.

"Okay then," she said smugly and sat back down.

My dad sat there with a stern look on his face. He glanced back and forth at me and Speedy, like he knew we were up to something and was trying to figure out exactly what it was. He seemed suspicious, like there was no way this could be as innocent as it looked. Meanwhile, Speedy was trying to appear calm, but his body was iron-stiff.

"So, Agapito," my mother said, "what do you do at the senior center?"

Speedy looked down at his plate. He was blushing badly. I wondered if he was nervous to be around my brothers and dad. They were so big and brawny next to Speedy.

Nana nudged him. "Come on Agapito," she said. "Don't be shy."

"I help with the fundraisers," Speedy mumbled while putting a spoonful of food into his mouth quickly.

"He bakes," my nana explained, patting him on the hand. "No shame in knowing how to make a good cheesecake," she said. "You know, Jesus' dad was a baker," Nana explained to my dad.

"Wasn't Jesus' dad a carpenter?" Bobby asked.

"Ugh!" Nana said, flustered. "He was a carpenter, too. But who do you think put food on the table, huh, Mr. Smarty Pants? *La Virgin* couldn't do everything by herself. She had the son of God to raise."

My brothers muffled their laughter as they ate.

Dad just shook his head and then he started to chuckle, softly at first, but then it grew into a full-blown belly laugh. He couldn't stop laughing, and tears came streaming down from his eyes onto the blue-and-green-checkered tablecloth.

I couldn't hold back either. The image of Speedy in a frilly apron baking cakes with a bunch of elderly ladies made me crack up.

My mother tried to hide her smile behind her paper napkin.

"So, where do you go to school?" my dad asked, after he regained his self-control. Now that we'd all had a laugh, everyone seemed a little bit more comfortable. Thank God for Nana.

"I'm at Mission," Speedy said quietly. He looked a bit unsure of himself. I couldn't help but wonder if he was lying.

My brothers looked up in surprise.

"I've never seen you there," Rey said in an accusatory tone. Sometimes he acted as if he were the mayor and knew every single person personally.

"Well, you see, I was out for a while." Speedy looked directly at me. "I didn't think school was my thing, but then *Señora de la Isla* convinced me to go back."

"That's my boy," Nana said, pinching his cheek. "I actually had to drag him there by the ear."

To my surprise, both Mom and Dad were smiling at each other. They hadn't done that in so long.

Rey shoved a second helping into his mouth. "Yo, Speedy, you know anything about cars?"

"Do I?" Speedy's eyes lit up. "I used to help out my old man every Sunday at the car shows."

"Your father competed?" my father asked. He seemed very interested in Speedy all of a sudden.

"Yeah, we used to drive all over for competitions. Fresno. Santa Monica. We had a customized '77 Ford pickup with hydraulics that won the hopping competitions two years in a row." I could see that my dad was impressed. He wiped his mouth clean with his napkin and pushed himself away from the table. "Let me show you what I got out back."

I smiled as Speedy and my father walked outside. Together.

My mother leaned toward me. "You know, it's too bad you're not having a *quinceañera*, because if you were, I think I know who your partner would be. Of course, I don't suppose it matters now. . . ."

I looked down, trying to hide my grin. Then I quickly glanced up at Nana to see if she'd given away my secret, but she was too busy taking out her dentures and trying to balance them on the top of her cup.

26

ajúa (a-'hoo-ah) n., Spanish, informal: 1. It means hurray! 2. a popular Northern Mexican shout. People usually yell it when they are real happy or encouraging someone. 3. also called a grito in Spanish

THERE WAS THIS ONE STRAND OF HAIR that wouldn't stay put, but Tere took care of it with some industrial-strength Aqua Net and some ultra-gooey pomade. My hair had been swirled up into some sort of very fancy twisty thing with little curls dangling down around my face. I'd even swiped the tiara from the top of my mother's dresser, and with the help of a few bobby pins it was now sparkling on top of my head.

Izzy had volunteered to do my makeup, but she was

under strict instructions not to make me look like a vampire, which she thankfully obeyed. The way she'd done my eyes with this shimmery champagne-colored shadow and my lips with this sparkling peach-colored gloss really made my entire face glow. And I was wearing the dress. The dreaded *quinceañera* dress. I had to admit, it truly looked beautiful. I couldn't believe it—after all the drama, it was finally the day of my *quince*!

Tere stormed into my room, shouting, "They're here! They're here!"

"Who?"

"Your parents," she replied.

I took a deep breath. There was a knot in my stomach the size of a fist, and I was practically shaking with excitement.

As I walked through the house, I heard a car door slam in the driveway. Then I took a deep breath and opened the front door. *Padrinos* and *madrinas* had arrived and were setting up for the big celebration. Nana was ordering her crew of senior ladies to set up the chairs. We'd borrowed them from practically everyone in the neighborhood, so none of them matched. Marta was busy hanging up decorations—silver streamers and pink and silver *quinceañera* balloons.

I looked at my parents, who were still unloading the El Camino. A few hours earlier we'd sent them off to the grocery store, with Bobby begging Mom to make her special chicken mole for dinner.

Dad was holding a few grocery bags. Mom was carrying a gallon of milk. But then she looked up, and our eyes locked.

There I was—all dolled up in my dress with my makeup and hair done and a crown on my head. "Surprise!" I shouted.

My mom stood there. Her jaw dropped open. I looked at my father, his eyes shining with tears. Both of them were staring at me as if they were just now seeing me for the very first time.

Then, slowly, I saw the understanding come over both of their faces as they realized what exactly was going on. My mother let out a scream and tossed the milk onto the ground. The container broke open, and milk flowed down the front steps. No one seemed to care. She threw her arms around me and hugged me so tightly, I could barely breathe.

"Watch the hair!" Tere called from inside the house.

"Oh, *mija!*" My mom touched my face and hair lightly, as if she didn't believe I was real. She turned toward my father. "Doesn't she look beautiful?" she asked.

My father beamed. "She really does."

"I never noticed until now how grown-up you are," she said. I'd been waiting so long to hear those words, and they filled me with pride.

My dad walked toward me. "You did all this by yourself?" He was shaking his head in disbelief.

"I had help."

"I thought you might be up to something," my mother said, her eyes open wide. "But never in a million years did I dream it would be this!"

The screen door slammed behind me. Nana, Tere, Izzy, Marta, and *Tía* Lucky, who was holding baby Maya in her arms, were standing there, smiling and waving.

"Lots of help."

"We're ready!" Bobby shouted, strutting out of the house. He was dressed to kill in a hot tuxedo that he'd borrowed from our neighbor Don Ramon (thankfully, it fit a lot better than the one he'd worn to Tere's *quince*). Rey darted out behind him with the confident swagger of an Armani runway model. My mother covered her mouth, she was in such shock. My brothers never dressed in anything other than jeans and T-shirts unless she "encouraged" them with the *chancla*.

Then everyone started laughing when Bill Clinton, Don Ramon's rooster, came out behind Rey wearing a bow tie. Actually, the bird strutted better than both of my brothers put together. Tere and Izzy had on matching hot pink gowns. Of course, Izzy wouldn't take off her combat boots, no matter how much I begged her to. But both of my girls were wearing their necklaces, and I was wearing mine.

There were some people missing, though. Some very important people who still hadn't forgiven me. But I tried to stay positive and count all the blessings I did have.

"Oh dear," my mom said, patting my dad's arm. "Everyone looks so nice."

Rey gave Tere a wink and she giggled.

Mom tugged on my dad's shirt excitedly. "C'mon, *viejo*. Let's get ready. We have a *quinceañera* to go to!"

"*Ajua!*" Izzy shouted. Everyone stepped aside to allow my parents in.

"*Mija*," my dad said as he pulled me aside. "How did you pay for all this?"

"Well, I asked a few people for some help. Apparently, when you ask people for what you need, sometimes they are glad to give it to you."

He was completely flabbergasted. "Wow, I am so proud of you, *mija!*"

We hugged, neither one of us able to hold back tears.

"Now hurry up and get dressed," I scolded. "I won't be late to my own *quince*."

My dad rushed inside.

I noticed that Tere was pacing back and forth in the driveway. She looked pretty with her hair twisted up—it made it much easier for people to see how her natural brown eyes shone so brightly (I'd been able to convince her to ditch those tinted contacts—they weren't her at all).

"Is everything all right?" I asked.

"Oh yeah, great," she said. "I'm just anxious, I guess."

Tere was definitely up to something sneaky, because she kept looking down the street as if she were expecting someone important. "What are you plotting, Teresa?"

"Me? Nothing," she said, shaking her head emphatically.

Tía Lucky grabbed my arm. She looked like such a diva in her red leopard-print dress and fuzzy black bolero jacket.

"Everything is better than perfect," she said and gave me a generous hug. Then I heard her sniffling.

"Come on, not you too, *Tía*. You're supposed to be the strong one, right?" I said.

"*Ah, mija,* I can't believe what you did. Thank you so much for inviting Marta," she said. "After our conversation I got to thinking about how hard I'd been on her and how much I missed my baby girl. I was stupid for trying to punish her by pushing her family away. I was going to call her but . . . Then I saw her with the babies this morning, and a flood of feelings overtook me. Temo is so big, and did you see Maya? That girl is going to be gorgeous. She takes after me, you know?"

I laughed and looked into her bright eyes.

"I was wrong, and I just hope she'll let me make it up to her."

I patted her gently on the back. "She'll forgive you. After all, we're *familia*." We stood there silently in a warm embrace, understanding each other completely.

No matter how hard the Alvarez family tried to be on time, we were always, *always* late. This time, we arrived at the church twenty minutes after the ceremony was to have started. Luckily, no one seemed upset with us.

A crowd of people started to cheer as we pulled up alongside the church in our cars. I was sitting in the backseat of my dad's lowrider, which he'd got running with the help of my brothers, who were in the van with my mom. Grand Master D was out front, instructing the guests to throw multicolored confetti at me when I came out of the car. There were so many members of my community here, people who I'd known all my life, staring at me proudly and applauding for me.

As I got out of the car, I searched the crowd for Izzy and Tere, who had left a little earlier than the rest of us, saying something about a surprise. I was pretty sure they were trying to find

Speedy for me. I didn't want to get my hopes up until I knew for sure, but just the thought of sharing this special day with him sent my heart pounding.

Someone started shouting, *"Felicidades!"* and the entire crowd roared their well-wishes. "Estrella! Estrella!" They were screaming out my name like I was a celebrity. My face turned red, and I wasn't sure I deserved so much attention. But what the hell—I had to admit it felt great. I felt like they were welcoming back the real me, and this time, she was definitely here to stay.

Grand Master D, who was looking especially classy in a white silk suit, took my hand and led me inside the church through a side door.

"Darling, you look wonderful." He leaned down and gave me a kiss on the cheek. "When your Nana told me what happened, I thought to myself, *Now this is one smart woman. I must help her in any way I can.*"

"Thank you so much, Grand Master D," I said. "I hope you don't mind, but we changed the dance a little bit."

"Estrella, darling. How can I mind? This is *your* day. Now, we must get you upstairs so you can make your big entrance," he said.

I was a bundle of nerves. Soon, everyone would have their eyes on me as I entered womanhood. I closed my eyes and said a silent prayer that Speedy would be there, too. And then I opened my eyes and—*Oh. My. God!*

Grand Master D had led me into the church foyer, and there, standing next to Tere and Izzy, were Christie and Sheila.

"Holy—!" I said. Then I covered my mouth.

Christie's hair was pulled back in a French twist. She was

wearing a pink tube dress with white strappy sandals. Sheila's brown locks were pulled back with blue barrettes that matched her off-the-shoulder cocktail dress. Christie's face was all flushed, and Sheila was biting her lip. Both of them looked nervous, like they weren't sure whether they'd be welcome at the party or not. It was probably just the way I'd looked at Tere's *quince*.

So I did what any good party host would do—I rushed over to them and hugged them as hard as I could.

"Star!" they cried out.

"I'm so glad you're both here," I said.

Christie's mascara was already dripping down her face. "You're so stunning!"

Sheila touched my dress and smiled. "Really, Star, I can't believe how incredible you look." Then she looked up at the tiara pinned to the top of my head. She grinned. "You're like a total rock star."

I turned around and saw Izzy and Tere watching us, both with huge grins on their faces. I turned back to Sheila and Christie. Christie's lips were pressed together. She opened and closed her mouth a few times like she wanted to speak but couldn't quite get the words out.

Sheila jumped in. "Listen, Star, this whole thing that happened, it's just stupid."

"We've been idiots," Christie said.

"Seriously," said Sheila. "Total bitch idiots."

"Total bitch idiots with fleas," Christie added.

"And tapeworms," Sheila put in.

"Okay, that's a little extreme." I laughed.

"We felt really terrible after the party," Christie said quietly. "Who knew Kevin was such a jerky loser? After you left, Kevin got even more drunk, and he tried to grab some other girl's ass. Only instead of slapping him, this girl went and got her giant boyfriend. Then the boyfriend and his friends threatened to beat the crap out of Kevin."

"And he was so scared, he peed his pants," Sheila said with a smirk.

"Seriously?" I let out a laugh. "Ha!"

Christie nodded emphatically. "Mark had to give him a ride home. And when Mark dropped Kevin off, he basically told him to go to hell. Which is what we should have told him after we talked to you in the bathroom. We would have come and talked to you about it, but we didn't know what to say. We were worried you'd hate us forever."

I was about to tell her that everything was fine, but she cut me off with a flip of her hand. I glanced over at Tere and she nodded.

"Let me finish." Christie took a deep breath while Sheila stood uncomfortably still next to her. "We thought that if Kevin was your boyfriend, you'd get a little ego boost and be happier. You seemed so uncomfortable all the time, like you were never quite sure whether you fit in. So we thought dating Kevin might make you feel better. We were just trying to help."

Sheila cleared her throat. "We never meant to make you feel bad about yourself or like we don't love you exactly how you are. You were totally right to go off on us at the party. I would've done the same thing if I'd been you. I thought about it later, and it was pretty badass that you slapped Kevin like that." She smiled, remembering the moment. "But let's get one thing straight: we would never, *ever* pity you. Look at what you have," she gestured with her arm.

"Look at how many people love you. And what great friends you have," Christie put in, with a small smile.

"We would never feel sorry for you, because there'd be no reason to," Sheila finished. "This, what you did here." Sheila was looking around at all the decorations and all the people. "I thought my fifteenth birthday was fun. But this is . . . amazing."

"Christie, Sheila," I said, taking their hands. "I'm sorry, too. I lied to both of you because I thought you wouldn't want to be my friend if I was more honest about everything. But it wasn't fair of me. I never gave you a chance. I was just going along with everything because I didn't know how to really stand up for what I wanted. I got so caught up in pleasing everyone, I forgot about me."

"Didn't I warn you about that?" Christie scolded.

"But really, Star. Will you ever be able to forgive us?" Sheila asked. For the first time, maybe ever, she looked totally serious. "Because we really love you and—"

"And I really love you guys, too," I said. I held my arms out, and the three of us hugged.

"I'm so glad I could be here to see you become a woman today," Sheila said with half a smirk. But her smile was genuine, and there were tears in her eyes.

"Yes," I said, solemnly. "Today I am a woman."

And all of us started giggling, like friends do.

Then I pointed at Izzy and Tere. "You two!"

Izzy pushed Tere in front of her. "She made me do it. It was all her idea."

Tere smiled with satisfaction. "C'mon, Estrella. You know you wanted them to come. You just couldn't admit it. So I had Izzy steal Christie's number from your cell."

"I'm glad you called," Christie said and pulled Tere into our little circle. "We wouldn't have missed this day for the world."

"I'm just sorry we couldn't help organize this party," Sheila said.

"We sure could have used your help," Izzy said, standing alongside Sheila. Their similarities became all too apparent just then. "Estrella's such a handful."

They all laughed. This was so amazing: my girls from Sacred Heart and the East Side were together and at my *quinceañera*.

"Christie, Sheila—do you want to be in my *quince*?" I asked.

Sheila looked at me as if I were nuts. "What are you talking about, crazy girl?"

"C'mon, guys. It'll be easy."

"But our dresses," Christie said. "We won't match."

"Guys." I laughed, hugging them both. "This is MY *quinceañera*. Nobody matches."

And then there was nothing left to do but hug, all of us together. I couldn't believe how lucky I felt. The only thing keeping me from being perfectly happy was that Speedy wasn't there. But I tried not to think about it. I knew I was very lucky at that moment because I was surrounded by so many people who cared about me. And that would have to be enough.

A few minutes later, as I stood in the entryway, I could hear the sound of mariachi-style music. We were just playing a CD, but it sounded just like the real thing. Nana handed me an old Bible she said had belonged to my grandfather and her rosary beads. I hugged her tightly.

Mom and Dad were the first to walk down the aisle. Mom looked beautiful in a cream-colored dress that she'd bought months ago at Nordstrom Rack. Dad looked handsome in the dark suit he wore for all special occasions. Then Rey walked down the aisle with Tere and Izzy, one on each arm, and a smirk on his face. Bobby was escorting Sheila and Christie, and he looked so excited, I was afraid he was going to burst.

Then it was just me. My heart was racing uncontrollably and I took a deep breath and stepped forward.

As I walked down the aisle, I was greeted by the bright smiles on everyone's faces. There was Margarita, sitting with her stocky husband, Hugo, and Mom's boss, Cassandra, seated with a bunch of the families from Head Start. There was my little neighbor Diego Lopez, bouncing up and down in his seat while his parents, Ernesto and Ana, tried to get him to sit still. *Tía* Lucky was holding both Temo and Maya on her lap. I'd never felt such joy in a room before.

Father Jim's Irish voice echoed throughout the entire hall as he began to welcome everyone in Spanish. He talked about how important this day was to Mexican people and how I was making the journey into womanhood. Then he asked me to read a passage.

Lord,

I stand before you in the best of health. I taste the joy of being alive and of possessing the goodwill of my relatives and friends. The future lies before me. Today, in complete freedom and with full knowledge, I offer to you all my wishes and plans. Take them as a gift. I place in your hands the offering of my life. I have only one request: grant me clarity and the courage to walk tall.

After the ceremony ended, I was surprised to find a group of Aztec dancers outside the church. Nana leaned over and told me that this was also a part of my family's tradition. A dark man with long black hair pounded fiercely on a wooden drum. The dancers moved effortlessly in brightly colored outfits and wore long feathers in their hair. Everyone stood silently, watching them in awe. They were all so graceful, so beautiful. But the prettiest one of all was Marta.

* 27 *

pachanga (pa-'chan-ga) n., Spanish, informal: 1. party! Any time family and friends get together to celebrate with good food and loud music. 2. term commonly used for house parties and not for formal events like weddings or baptisms

THE OJOS DE DIOS CLAN HAD DONE A FABULOUS JOB of decorating our backyard with leftover streamers and balloons, which had been supplied by Juana's store. It looked so festive and cheery.

Already guests were arriving and placing gifts around the cake table. Marta's husband, Suave, was up in his DJ stand. As soon as we all entered, he put on some beats. Nana immediately got her groove on when 50 Cent's "In Da Club" came on full blast. Suave was still tinkering with the sound system when Grand Master D and I came up to him. I gave him a nod and he passed the mike to Grand Master D. It was time to begin the show.

It was a rowdy crowd. Guests were laughing loudly, catching up with lifelong friends as if it were a high school reunion. Grand Master D patted the mike a few times to get their attention.

He cleared his throat loudly.

"*Buenas tardes*," he said. "I want to thank everyone for coming here on this special day to honor Estrella Alvarez on her fifteenth birthday. My name is Grand Master D, *quinceañera* choreographer, and I will be your host for the evening."

As the crowd applauded, I went over all the dance steps in my mind. There were some turns and fancy moves, which Bobby had insisted on putting in. I had practiced all week, but I still felt really self-conscious about performing in front of a large group of people. I glanced over at Marta. She was sweating a little bit from the exertion of chasing her toddler while carrying a baby in her arms. She had the CD out, ready to go. I had chosen, the song "Sleepwalker" from the movie *La Bamba*, and DJ Suave had helped out by adding some hip-hop San Jose flavor to it.

Then the music began. An electric guitar played a heart-wrenching melody. Tere, Izzy, and I took our places on one side of the temporary dance floor that had been laid over the dirt in our backyard. Bobby and Rey were lined up on the opposite side, smiling. The five of us danced around in a circle. We twirled once, got into a line, and twirled again. I was worried that Tere would turn the wrong way, but because I was looking at her, I totally missed my turn. Bobby snickered. Our eyes locked and he tensed up, but then I burst out laughing, too.

Still, I finished the dance without hurting myself or anyone else. Once it ended, the audience erupted in cheers and shouted, "Bravo." I looked out into the crowd to find Grand Master D, but I couldn't see him. I hoped that he wasn't too pissed at us for switching all of his moves around. Just then, I smelled Tres Flores, and someone picked me up from behind and twirled me around.

"That was magnificent," I heard a voice whisper in my ear. "Why didn't you tell me you could dance like that?"

Speedy was standing right there in front of me, smiling. He was wearing the most perfect pinstriped zoot suit with a UFW eagle pinned to his lapel. He gazed deeply into my eyes.

"There are a lot of things you don't know about me," I said. All the background party noises faded, and he was all I could hear and all I could see. It was just me and Speedy.

"That's why I'm here," he said. He brushed my neck lightly with the tips of his fingers. "I thought about what you said—that you had learned a lot and wanted the chance to prove it to me. Well, Estrella Alvarez, I'd like to get to know everything about you, if you'll let me."

"What about my father?"

"I don't think that'll be a problem," he said with a smile. "When I was out back with your dad the other night, he said I should come over to help with the Impala anytime I wanted. He also said that maybe he'd one day let me take you out to dinner in it."

I blinked. "He really said that?"

Speedy nodded. "But then he said if I ever caused you any trouble, he'd unleash your mom on me with that *chancla* of hers, and he could not be responsible for what she might do."

I let out a laugh. "That sounds more like him."

"It's a start," he said. "This is just the beginning." Speedy stood there grinning at me, and he looked so damn cute.

So I did something, right there in the middle of the dance floor, in front of everyone: I pulled Speedy toward me by the lapels of his jacket. He was so close to me that our noses were touching. Speedy laughed. "I guess the birthday girl wants a kiss?"

As his soft lips gently touched mine, I closed my eyes and breathed him in, a gust of roses in the air. Then suddenly, I was in one of those rare moments where time seems to stand still and everything is perfect. But this was my *quinceañera,* so of course it didn't last long. A couple seconds later, I heard lots of yelling over the low bass of a Missy Elliott song.

"Get out of the way!"

"Everyone move!"

"Hurry! Hurry!"

Speedy and I broke from our embrace. We looked around, confused. What was going on?

Then I saw Bobby behind the wheel of our lowrider, Chava, which was heading toward us. It was bouncing up and down a foot off the ground and gaining speed with each jump of the hydraulics.

It was so out of control that it had guests screaming for their lives, but then it veered away from the dining area and bounced right into the table that held my birthday cake.

Splat, it went, all over the floor. At least Chava was finally brought to a halt.

Rey ran over behind me and Speedy. "I'm really sorry, Estrella."

He sounded sincere. He really did look like he felt bad, but in my opinion, not bad enough.

So I did the only thing a girl—no, scratch that, a *woman*—could do: I reached out, grabbed a handful of cake, and slammed it directly into his face.

"Hey!" he cried. "I just wanted the car to dance to the music!" He grabbed a big fistful of cake. "Congratulations, Estrella." He pushed the cake against my cheek. Tere, Izzy, Christie, and Sheila screamed and ran over. They each grabbed a chunk of cake and tossed it at Rey. Then Bobby joined in too.

Suddenly, Speedy tapped me on the shoulder, a big glob of icing in his hand. "For old times' sake," he said, and then dropped it on top of my head. He let out a maniacal laugh and started to trot away.

"I guess I was wrong about what I said, Speedy," I called out. "I think I *will* chase you." I ran after him with a giant piece of cake in my hand. Dad was laughing so hard watching us that he didn't even notice Bobby coming up from behind. *Bam!* More cake in the face. Everyone thought this was hilarious, even my mother, who was laughing so hard, she was crying.

"This is part of our family's tradition," Tere explained to Christie as she licked icing off her wrist.

"I love it," Sheila said. "Your tradition is delicious."

They smiled at each other.

This is how it should have been from the beginning, I thought.

Then I heard my mom's voice beckoning me from the microphone. "Estrella?"

I hitched up my dress, kicked off the heels that had been pinching my toes, and raced over to her.

My mother was holding the microphone in one hand and a glass of champagne in the other. "Come say a few words before the toast, *mija*." I walked over to her and she gave me a big kiss.

Once I'd straightened my dress and wiped the cake off my forehead, I smiled at my friends and family. Then I breathed in deep and spoke from my soul.

"First of all, I'd like to thank everyone for coming out here today." I took another deep breath and looked out into the crowd of smiling, happy faces. And then I had a sudden strange moment of clarity—*I am at my* quinceañera. *This is what it has all been about. This is it.* I felt a warmth rush up the back of my spine, and I continued. "None of this could have been possible without the support and love of each of you." My eyes landed on Margarita, *Tía* Lucky, Nana, the Gonzalezes, the Lopezes, the Ortizes, the Veras, the Talamanteses, the Dominguezes, and everyone else. They were all beaming at me and I went on. "I especially want to thank all the *madrinas* and *padrinos* who helped put together this reception. My homegirls: Izzy, Tere, Sheila, and Christie. You guys have taught me the true meaning of friendship. To my bros, Bobby and Rey, thanks for putting up with me. And to Speedy," I blushed, thinking of how I couldn't wait to kiss him again. "Just . . . thanks."

Speedy looked at me and winked.

"And to my amazing parents: Mom, you're the best. You taught me to have pride in myself, in my culture, and in my family. And Dad, you've taught me the meaning of sacrifice and humility." I paused and blinked. The tears were on their way. I just hoped I could get through my speech first. "I used to think that I had to hide different parts of myself from everyone, only showing people what I thought they wanted to see. I used to think my happiness depended on my never disagreeing with anyone. But what I've come to realize is that you *have* to be yourself, because you can never be anyone else. If people truly care about you, they will accept all the different pieces and parts of you and love you for exactly who you are. I want us all to fit in, together, as one big family. I hope you'll all join me in this journey into adulthood. I promise to make you all proud, and most of all, to take pride in myself!"

The crowd cheered. Someone started shouting "*¡Viva Estrella!*" I looked over and saw Sheila, Christie, Izzy, and Tere prompting the crowd. So I joined in, responding, "*Viva!*" with everyone else.

Then Suave put the music back on, and everyone got up to get their groove on.

I found all my friends on the dance floor. Tere was shaking her booty for Rey. Bobby was doing a pathetic Elvis hip-gyrating impersonation, but Sheila and Izzy were cheering him on and slapping his butt. Christie was getting private *cumbia* lessons from Grand Master D. I glanced over at my *tía* Lucky. She was sitting at Marta's table with Suave and little Temo. My *tía* was doting over her granddaughter, giddily bouncing the little girl on her knee. Marta came up behind her mother and hugged her affectionately. *Tía* Lucky then kissed her precious child on the cheek.

As for me, I couldn't wipe the smile off my face. My heart was overflowing with love for all the people I cared about most, who were all together in one place. I looked over to where

Speedy stood in the center of the dance floor, waiting for me, his hand outstretched.

When he took me in his arms, I held him tightly and whispered into his ear, "*Este día no podia ser más perfecto.*"

This day couldn't be more perfect.

spanglish 101

Glossary of Spanish-to-English terms
in order of appearance

quinceañera a young woman's fifteenth birthday party

estrella star

fiesta party

cha cha anything tacky and big

mija my daughter (short for mi hija)

bribón scoundrel

señora lady, Mrs.

tía aunt

padrinos godfathers

mariachis traditional Mexican band

bolero slow romantic Mexican music

carnitas traditional Mexican dish uses pork, cilantro, cumin, and onion served with corn tortillas

barrio neighborhood

hola hello

chancla slipper

weenie con huevo weenies with eggs

paletero pushcart Popsicle vender

cholo thug, gangster

chica girl

macho manly, tough guy

chancla house slipper

a ver let's see

mira look here

el rey the king

chorizo Mexican sausage

fresita preppy

fresa literal meaning, strawberry; inferred meaning, stuck up

lobo wolf

mijo my son (short for mi hijo)

papá Dad

mensa stupid

banda band or lively dance music

fufu rufu gaudy

nuestra belleza our beauty

Cinco de Mayo Fifth of May

dama unwed woman

panadero baker

pan dulces Mexican sweet bread

ranchera country music

pues well

ojos de Dios eyes of God

mijita my little girl

maestro teacher

familia family

mestizaje refers to mixture of Spanish and Indian culture/blood

chambelan escort to the dance

quesadilla tortilla and cheese snack

pena shame or embarrassment

recuerdo a reminder or party favor

la cucaracha a cockroach

qué pasa? what's up?

carnala "homegirl" or best friend

chiquita little one

escándalo scandal

nalgas buttocks

carne asada marinated grilled steak

mal de ojo a spell

eso, eso, eso right on, that's it

sabes qué you know what?

el peludo the hairy one, the daring one

flaco slim

caldo de res beef/vegetable soup

doña/don grand lady or man

mole chocolate and chile sauce for meat or chicken dish

muñeca doll

chamaca girl

no quiero esto en mi casa! I don't want this in my house!

ay viejo oh, honey

trio three musicians who sing boleros

hijole expression similar to "Oh my God!"

vago vagabond

la raza the people, referring to mixed-race Latinos

entiendes? do you understand?

vendida sellout

ay mamacita sexy mama

tequila alcoholic drink from Mexico

confianza trust

sorpresa surprise

menudo soup made of tripe, hominy, and chili

sarape blanket or shawl

telenovela soap opera

qué te pasa? what's wrong with you?

no me oyes? don't you hear me?

nopales cactus

bronca fight

terca stubborn

perdón forgiveness

sí se puede yes you can

chismosa gossiper

ajúa hooray!

felicidades congratulations

pachanga party

buenas tardes good evening

ACKNOWLEDGMENTS

I am grateful to the many people who came together to breathe life into this book. *Muchisimas gracias* to my fabulous editors Claudia Gabel, David Gale, and all the peeps at Alloy Entertainment and Simon & Schuster for believing in this project. Thank you for your flexibility and humor throughout this adventure. (*Mujer*, we did it!)

I want to thank my homegirls and all the *vatos locos* from Manhatitlan to Cali, *Las Nopalitas*, the Lovefest chulas, WILL, Cetiliztli and all the members of my extended family. Their *cariño*, late-night drinks at Bob's and endless support helped me complete *este proyecto*. Thanks to my dear friends Pena and Ish for helping me stay sane, and to Angelina and MJ for sharing their homes so that I could work without distractions (You saved me, *chicas!*). *Mil abrazos* to Jennie *y la familia Luna* for their encouragement, *cuentos*, and for sharing their *barrio conmigo*.

Thanks to my mom, *la mera chingona*, for all the blissful childhood memories of flying *chanclas* and Sundays at *la pulga*, for her tireless edits, massages, and all her motherly advice. Much love to Kiki, Lucy, Jelly, and Bill for being the best cheerleaders a girl could ask for. Thanks to my dad for teaching me the meaning of hard work and persistence. And special thanks to my little sis, Suni Serena, for not following in her older sisters' footsteps and demanding her own puffy-dressed, *fufu rufu quinceañera*. I'm proud of the woman she has become (*Ajua!*).

ABOUT THE AUTHOR

Malín Alegría is an accomplished educator, dancer, and actress who has co-written and performed in several stage plays. She also writes poetry and short stories. Malín lives in San Francisco. This is her first novel.